Cosmas
or the Love of God

Books in the Loyola Classics Series

Cosmas
or the Love of God

PIERRE DE CALAN

Translated by Peter Hebblethwaite

Introduction by James Martin, SJ

LOYOLA CLASSICS

CHICAGO

LOYOLAPRESS.

3441 N. ASHLAND AVENUE
CHICAGO, ILLINOIS 60657
(800) 621-1008
WWW.LOYOLAPRESS.ORG

First published as *Côme ou le désir de Dieu* by Editions de la Table Ronde, Paris

First published in Great Britain 1980

Library of Congress Catalog Card Number: 80-508
First American edition: 1980

Series art direction: Adam Moroschan
Series design: Adam Moroschan and Erin Van Werden
Cover design: Mia Basile
Interior design: Erin Van Werden

Library of Congress Cataloging-in-Publication Data
Calan, Pierre de, 1911–
    [Côme. English]
    Cosmas, or, The love of God / Pierre de Calan; translated by Peter
Hebblethwaite.
        p. cm. — (Loyola classics series)
    ISBN-13: 978-0-8294-2395-2
    ISBN-10: 0-8294-2395-8
        I. Hebblethwaite, Peter. II. Title. III. Title: Cosmas. IV. Title:
Love of God. V. Series.
PQ2672.A347C613 2006
843'.914—dc22
                                                        2006010617

Printed in the United States of America
06 07 08 09 10 11 Versa 10 9 8 7 6 5 4 3 2 1

Introduction

James Martin, SJ

A few years ago, an elderly priest in my Jesuit community heard my confession one night after dinner. For the life of me, I can't remember what I confessed, but after my friend gave me a suitable penance and pronounced the ritual words of absolution, he said, "I have a book that I think you should read."

After rooting around in his overstuffed bookshelves, he produced a copy of Pierre de Calan's novel *Cosmas or the Love of God*. It was a hardbound edition of the first English translation, masterfully done in 1980 by the English Catholic writer and journalist Peter Hebblethwaite. Though I had read dozens of books on monastic life on my way to entering a religious order, I had never heard of the novel or its author. The stark white cover, torn in places, showed a portrait of a sad-faced man clad in a brown habit, standing with hands outstretched.

"Please don't lose it," said my friend. He explained that his only copy, its pages yellowing with age, had once been lost in someone else's collection for some time, and that he had taken great pains to retrieve it.

The book is the story of a young man's passionate desire to enter a Trappist monastery in 1930s France. After finishing it, I wondered what prompted the priest to recommend the book, for the main character, Cosmas—a pious man with a painful family background—struggles mightily with trying to understand his vocation. His tale is told by Father Roger, the monastery's former novice master, or person responsible for training the monastery's newest members. Throughout the novel, Cosmas questions not simply if he is "called" to monastic life but, more important, if he *is* called, whether he can live out his vocation faithfully, or at all.

The questions upon which the novel turns are: What is a vocation? Is a vocation something that you feel God is calling you to do? And, if you feel drawn to a particular vocation but discover that you cannot do it, does it follow that God is now asking you *not* to do it?

Whole lives—single, married, vowed, ordained—have been spent pondering those difficult questions. Does unhappiness in a religious community mean that one should leave? Or is fidelity and perseverance the answer? Likewise, does unhappiness in a job, in a friendship, or in a marriage mean that one should switch careers, sever a relationship, or even end a marriage? This is Cosmas's dilemma. As the narrator asks, "[W]as Cosmas really called to religious life? No other question has ever disturbed me so much."

By the time I asked my confessor what it was about the book that had reminded him of my own situation, he had already forgotten. (One grace of good confessors is the ability to forget the content of confessions.) So I was forced to seek meaning in the book on my own.

After several readings, with my appreciation for the book deepening each time, the tale of the young novice began to offer me new ways of understanding the mystery of living out a vocation and, more specifically, living out a vocation in a religious community.

There is an irony in this. Monsieur de Calan, who died in 1993, was neither a Trappist nor a priest nor a member of a religious order. Born in Paris in 1911, he studied philosophy and mathematics and worked for many years as a tax inspector, eventually becoming president of the French division of the prestigious Barclays Bank. At the time of the first printing of *Côme ou le désir de Dieu* in 1977, Calan was married with six children and eighteen grandchildren. The story of the businessman publishing a timeless novel is reminiscent of the American poet Wallace Stevens who, when not writing poetry, worked as an executive in an insurance company in Hartford, Connecticut. As Peter Hebblethwaite says in the introduction to the first English edition, there is no reason that a businessperson cannot be literate as well as numerate.

Still, Pierre de Calan's achievement is as unlikely as a celibate priest writing a convincing portrait of married life.

While the author has a firm grasp of the complexities of Trappist life, readers of his book may not be as familiar with them, so perhaps some background is in order.

In 1098, a group of monks left the Benedictine abbey at Molesmes, in France, to live a more stringent version of the Rule of St. Benedict. They continued to pray several times a day, lived in extremely simple conditions, and engaged in manual labor, typically on their own farms, to feed and support themselves. Their first community was located in the town of Cîteaux, and from the Latin version of its name, *Cistercium*, came the name of the new order: the Cistercians.

Over the next few decades the order established new communities across Europe, each headed by an "abbot" (from the Aramaic word *abba*, meaning father). By the middle of the twelfth century, there were 333 abbeys for men; a century later there were 647. Houses for lay brothers and for nuns also became part of the larger Cistercian family.

By the seventeenth century, some Cistercians felt the need to return to the originally strict observance of the Rule. The most influential of these abbeys was headed by Armand Jean Le Bouthillier de Rancé, and located in La Trappe, France, the very same monastery where *Cosmas* is set. In 1893, three of these groups—"at papal insistence" according to the *Encyclopedia of Catholicism*—were gathered together as the Order of Cistercians of the Strict Observance, popularly known as "Trappists," after the abbey of Rancé.

As late as the mid-twentieth century, life in a Trappist monastery varied little from what Rancé had intended. One window into this world is offered by the writings of the American Trappist Thomas Merton, who entered the Abbey of Our Lady of Gethsemani in the hills of Kentucky in 1941, just a few years after the fictional Cosmas entered his in La Trappe.

Merton's autobiography, *The Seven Storey Mountain*, as well as the journal of his early years in the monastery, published as *The Sign of Jonas*, describe practices and procedures that are literally medieval. The monks work in the fields with the simplest of tools, their carts and plows drawn by horses. They eat plain food, fast for much of the year, maintain silence for most of the day, and sleep in unheated dormitories while fully clothed in their woolen habits. (Some of the bluntest passages in Merton's journals come when he describes the torment of wearing those heavy woolen habits during the humid Kentucky summers.)

They also gather to pray, something that Trappists are still doing around the world. The daily prayers of the Divine Office, the combination of psalms and readings from Scripture that are mostly chanted, are still the mainstay of the church's monastic orders. In the Trappist abbey in Kentucky, for example, the first prayer of the day, Vigils, still begins at 3:15 a.m., and the last,

Compline (so called because it "completes" the day), comes at 7:30 p.m. Following the age-old patterns of the medieval life, which are tethered to the rising and the setting of the sun, the schedule is a rigorous one.

It is not the physical difficulties that plague Cosmas, however, as much as the spiritual ones. The young man enters the monastery joyfully, in the full bloom of what is often called "first fervor." Nothing is too hard; all seems full of light. It is similar to the beginning of any relationship: a period of infatuation is perfectly natural. Gradually, though, most members of religious orders discover—as do couples and spouses—that the object of their affection is not perfect. For Cosmas, this recognition assumes an unusual form: he finds it unseemly that the monks are so concerned with the business end of running a monastery. (He seems to have forgotten that monks need to eat and earn a living like everyone else.)

"I expected," Cosmas tells Father Roger with disappointment, "to find a greater difference between those who remain in the world and those who spend long hours in prayer and whose lives are dedicated to God's service."

There is something even more troubling for Cosmas and, by extension, for his novice master: Cosmas cannot accept the fact that his brother Trappists are so human. One quarrels loudly and violently with another; one pilfers chocolates from the common pantry. After just a few months in the monastery, Cosmas is tormented by the inadequacies—the humanity—of his fellow monks.

It was here, on my first reading of *Cosmas*, that I remembered my early need to confront this part of life in a religious community, which again mirrors a phenomenon encountered in all relationships. The person you love, the community you love, is always flawed. One person can be argumentative. Another can be lazy. Another can even be cruel at times. At first this was shocking. When I was a Jesuit novice, one of Thomas Merton's comments helped me respond to the same emotions that Cosmas felt:

> The first and most elementary test of one's call to the religious life—whether as a Jesuit, Franciscan, Cistercian, or Carthusian—is the willingness to accept life in a community in which everybody is more or less imperfect.

Moreover, holiness, as Father Roger tells Cosmas, is not something that we attain instantaneously. The imperfections of the community and of the other person are to be expected, and are, since they reveal our weaknesses, reminders of our reliance on God. Nor does sanctity mean perfection: even the saints were not perfect. Rather, holiness, as the novice master explains, is "a distant goal toward which, day by day, they inch forward with humility and constant effort—rather like the mountaineer whose upward progress is so slow."

While this realization eludes Cosmas, for the attentive and receptive reader it arrives as both a relief and a challenge. Sanctity is attainable even for flawed individuals. Holiness consists in becoming the person who God created, not some dry, desiccated copy of a plaster saint. As Merton wrote, "For me to be a saint means to be myself." This realization also seems to elude Cosmas.

Pierre de Calan's novel is not simply about Cosmas, however. In many ways, it is as much about Father Roger, the wise novice master, who acts as a foil for the young monk. Where Cosmas is impatient, the novice master is patient. Where he has little use for the inadequacies of others, the novice master is infinitely forgiving. And where Cosmas fails to trust, Father Roger invests others with complete trust.

In this way, the narrator embodies the second part of the book's title, *the Love of God*. Indeed, one of the joys of reading *Cosmas* is that by the end of the book one feels that one has spent time with two superb spiritual directors and two loving men: Father Roger and the austere but ultimately compassionate abbot, Dom Philippe.

A further word about the title, *Cosmas or the Love of God*. In the end, Pierre de Calan's book is really about the love of

God: the love that seeks out Cosmas and urgently calls him to religious life; the love that impels the novice master to support Cosmas even when the novice seems deaf to his advice; the love that enables the abbot to give Father Roger the freedom to make his own decisions; the love that draws the young man back to the abbey, over and over; and the final and beautiful expression of love shown by the entire community to their wandering brother, Cosmas.

God's love embraces all these characters in all these situations, as it does in real lives. "Mercy within mercy within mercy," wrote Thomas Merton—and this, I think, is something of what he must have meant.

James Martin, SJ, is a Jesuit priest and associate editor of America *magazine. His most recent book is* My Life with the Saints, *a memoir published by Loyola Press.*

Cosmas
or the Love of God

Translator's Introduction

Peter Hebblethwaite

It is unnecessary and indeed presumptuous to come between the author and the reader of *Cosmas or the Love of God*. The book either speaks for itself or it does not. Having lived with it for well over a year, I believe that it does speak eloquently, soberly (to use one of the author's favorite words), and effectively. To come across a French novel that is concerned neither with human love nor sexual combinations nor revolution nor the impossibility of saying anything, but with the quest for God in religious life, is in itself a sufficiently startling departure from convention to raise eyebrows and arouse interest. But a few words of explanation may be useful for those who are intrigued by the novel and curious about its author.

Pierre de Calan is not a Cistercian monk. Nor has he ever been a novice at La Trappe, which exists, just as he describes it, not far from Soligny in Le Perche. The Cistercians began in 1098 as a group of monks who wanted to keep the Rule of St. Benedict in all its rigor. They take their name from the Latin version of their first foundation at Cîteaux (*Cistercium*) in Burgundy. When St. Bernard joined the Cistercians in 1113 they began to expand rapidly all around Europe, and by his death in 1153 there were more than three hundred Cistercian houses. Decline, not in numbers but in quality of monastic life, set in as the Reformation approached. In France their post-Reformation reformer was the formidable Abbé de Rancé, who restored the ancient discipline in the seventeenth century. Chateaubriand wrote about his life on the orders of his spiritual director. It was his last, and most moving, work.

Pierre de Calan's book shows so much insight into Cistercian life that many have concluded that he must have written from direct experience. At a presentation of *Cosmas* in Paris, Calan's wife heard two army officers discussing him. They agreed that he must be an "unfrocked Trappist" and the only argument was about how long he spent there: estimates varied between three months and three years. False though this is, it is a tribute to the authenticity of his detail and atmosphere.

In fact, Pierre de Calan is president of Barclays Bank in France and has held important posts in the *Patronat Français*—the equivalent of the Confederation of British Industry. He finds it odd that people should wonder why a banker should publish his first novel at the age of sixty-six. "A man who lives only for his work," he says, "leads a half life." Apart from books on economic questions such as the cotton market and the perennial topic of inflation, he had already published a volume of short stories, *Les cousins vraisemblables* (H. Lefebvre), and in 1959 he worked with Michel de Saint-Pierre on the stage version of the latter's novel, *Les écrivains* (Grasset). There is no reason why a banker should not be literate as well as numerate.

Calan's fascination with La Trappe and monastic life dates back to his childhood, when he spent much of his time in the village of Bonsmoulins, not far from Soligny. The abbey, with its three lakes, its forests, its farm, its changing seasons, is not invented: it is La Trappe de Soligny. The three principal characters—Cosmas himself; Father Roger, the novice master; and Dom Philippe Jalluy, the abbot—are fictions. But the setting and landscapes are authentic, and the terrifying Brother Sébastien, who could thunder in silence, really existed. He is a boyhood memory.

In discussion, Pierre de Calan cleared up a number of points about the form of the book. It is a first-person novel, and the narrator, novice master at the time of the Cosmas episode, later becomes abbot—but we discover that only at the end of the book. We then learn for the first time his name: Dom Roger. He is of a working-class family from Cambrai in northern France. He is garrulous—a compensation for monastic silence?—occasionally repetitive, lyrical at times, inclined to embark on didactic digressions, easily moved by the beauty of nature, and above all obsessed by the mystery of Cosmas's vocation, if it were a vocation. Can someone really be called by God and not have the right dispositions to answer this call? And, more generally, how does God regard those whom we are inclined to write off as failures? By using a first-person narrative, Calan adopts a limited point of view. This means that Father Roger should not be identified with Pierre de Calan; and that we only see events through the eyes of Father Roger. We do not, for example, discover what Cosmas really thinks "from the inside," except through the letters that are quoted. I asked Calan why he had chosen this indirect form. Bernanos, he replied, might have written such a novel as a quasi-omniscient narrator, "but I, Pierre de Calan, could not say these things—I needed the intercession of a monk."

Written, then, from the point of view of the novice master, the novel is also addressed to a specific individual. The addressee is an unbeliever, a friend who has spent some weeks at the guesthouse of La Trappe and who is fascinated by these lives lived wholly for God. Monastic life challenges the values and conventional wisdoms of the modern world. It presupposes that the monk is prepared to stake his entire life on the reality and overriding importance of God. In human terms it makes little sense. So either it points to God or it is an illusion. This is where the addressee comes in: we are never told how the two met. There is a hint that perhaps they were at school together (Father Roger recalls an experiment in physics class). But perhaps the "friend" just turned up at La Trappe. In any case it does not matter, for the function of the addressee is to represent the reader, without ever preempting his responses. The addressee also introduces the possibility of doubt. "You may find what I am saying exaggerated or mistaken," says Father Roger more than once; but this allowing for skepticism serves to heighten the credibility of the novel.

Cosmas is set in the past, and February 1938 is given as the most probable date for Cosmas's death. I asked Calan why he had chosen this distant, prewar setting. His answer was that he had not wanted to get embroiled in the postconciliar discussions on "changes in the church" that have not left monastic life unscathed. But since, however, the narrator is writing in the present or near present, the picture of monastic life is not notably out of date and the changes that have been introduced by the Cistercians are carefully noted. The main ones are that there is a one-hour discussion after the evening meal (more usually and accurately known as *collation*), that the chapter of faults at which one could accuse oneself and others has been abolished, that the distinction between choir monks and lay brothers no longer exists, and that attendance at Divine Office is no longer compulsory—though everyone continues to go. In short, the distancing in time permits a calmer approach to the abiding problem of a religious vocation, which is the central theme of the book.

One French publisher, who to his subsequent chagrin rejected the novel, complained that all suspense had been abolished by identifying the body and the approximate circumstances of death right from the start. A detective novel can have a body in its opening chapter, but too much should not be given away too soon, and the clues should gradually be laid before the reader. But Georges Simenon is not the only norm for the detective novel. Bernanos, in *Un crime,* had shown that one can start from an identifiable body and an identified murderer with no lack of suspense: but the interest then shifts away from whodunit to why he did it. The same principle holds here, and one could no doubt evoke Gabriel Marcel's distinction between a puzzle and a mystery: a puzzle does not involve me or my feelings, it lies objectively there, and resolving it is not a matter of life and death; but a mystery engages my attention and my feelings in such a way that I have to respond to it. Seen in these terms, *Cosmas* is not so much a puzzle as a mystery, and a mystery that takes one into regions of the spirit that normally lie outside the confines of a novel. "The mind," as Gerard Manley Hopkins sang, "the mind has mountains, dark sheer, no-man-fathomed."

Many critics have been able to follow Father Roger into this mysterious realm. Some—including the most unlikely—have been enthusiastic. Thus, André Stil of the French Communist Party praised it for the way it made sense of "the search for the absolute." Armand Salacrou, of the Académie Goncourt, confessed that he was *bouleversé* (overwhelmed) on reading it. When it appeared in 1977, *Cosmas* was considered for the Prix Goncourt and made the last selection of sixteen novels. But as Pierre de Calan remarked, not without humor, "it had little hope of winning the prize, since the Goncourt is meant to encourage young writers, and here I am with six children and already eighteen grandchildren." But French television is making a film of *Cosmas.*

More interesting than what literary critics or media types think about *Cosmas* is the response of the Cistercian monks themselves. They can say better than anyone else whether Calan has captured or travestied their way of life. For them the nature of a religious vocation is not an idle speculation or a literary poser: they are in it for real. *Cosmas* was submitted to the ultimate test: it was read aloud in the refectory at La Trappe de Soligny, and after the reading the monks discussed it with the author. A letter from Dom Marie Gérard, the real-life abbot of La Trappe, summarizes their impressions. The abbot was wholly delighted and quoted a theologian who said that so much theology could be conveyed through novels. Had not Hans Urs von Balthasar, one of the most outstanding Roman Catholic theologians of the century, written a fat volume on the novels of Georges Bernanos? "I am struck," wrote the abbot, "by your literary success in holding the attention of the reader throughout the 219 pages of your book, and by the psychological and theological analysis of the criteria for a vocation. You tackle the subject head-on and maintain the interest in a way which theological textbooks signally fail to do." Father Marie Gérard, like the narrator in *Cosmas,* was first novice master and is now abbot. This "ideal reader" concludes: "As I read your book, I have to admit that I kept saying, 'Yes, that's just the way it is.'"

Only on two points is Dom Marie Gérard mildly critical. He finds Cosmas's insistence on the certainty of his vocation slightly dubious, given that he is never prepared to consider what the abbot or the novice master think about it. He goes on: "It is true that those who have a genuine vocation feel quite sure about it and have an inner certainty, but paradoxically they need and want *recognition* on the part of those who are responsible for their vocation, and they remain unsure about the authenticity of their vocation so long as they do not have this recognition. It is an odd thing that those who are most sure of their vocation *despite* and *against* superiors are usually in illusion. To such an extent that obstinacy becomes evidence of a nonvocation. That links up with the theological pattern: God calls—and the church calls (the lives of saints always show a *humility* that makes them ready to question even their profoundest interior convictions)."

Dom Marie Gérard in his letter also reflected another criticism that came in the first instance from the novices at La Trappe. The emphasis on religious life as the fulfillment of the Rule seemed to them to be misleading. Although they conceded that the love of God in fact led to a passionate fidelity to the Rule of St. Benedict, they wanted to dispel the impression that "monastic life *consists in* obeying orders for the rest of one's days. That is too much like the 'military discipline' that Father Roger wants to avoid. And that shocks young people: one does not come here *in order* to keep the Rule and to obey the orders of superiors. It is true that 'regularity' was at one time in the forefront of our spirituality, and of course it presupposed the love of God. But the framework and foundation of religious life must not become the most important aspect of it. Today we lay greater stress on the positive *values* lived out in monastic life than on the context of regularity in which they take place. 'Regularity' by itself seems cold and comes to resemble some kind of Kantian 'duty'."

But these two points aside—and by making them, the abbot showed that *Cosmas* was worth taking seriously—he congratulated the author on his perceptiveness and saluted him finally as "a monk and novice master *honoris causa* of La Trappe" (Letter to Pierre de Calan, 30 December 1977).

There could be no higher commendations. As a genre, the novel of monastic life has barely existed in France (or elsewhere for that matter). The reason is simply that monks are men of silence who do not feel impelled to write novels; and their "thoughts" or "lights" are confined to notebooks that are invariably destroyed on their death. The result is that religious life, when it has been considered at all, has been written about by outsiders with axes to grind. This is true whether one looks at hostile tracts from the eighteenth century, such as Diderot's *La Religieuse* or Chateaubriand's romantic conception of religious houses as hospitals for those bruised by an impossible love, or late nineteenth-century aesthetic Catholics such as Huysmans in *Là-bas,* who exploited monastic life as a stick with which to belabor the unheeding contemporary world. Even Bernanos, from whom Calan, with his conversations that are dialogues of salvation, is remotely descended, confined himself to studying diocesan priests whose lugubrious parishes were a microcosm of early twentieth-century France. To have written a successful novel about monastic life, a regional novel of the Spirit, is not the least of Calan's achievements. There was a gap. It has now been filled.

But it would be mistaken, in conclusion, simply to reduce *Cosmas* to a novel about monastic life. It is indeed that, but it is something else besides. Monks are related to the rest of the Christian community. They are not isolated eccentrics.

And an abbey is a place where the Christian life is lived to the full, with an intensity and an awareness not found elsewhere (which is why when it goes wrong, it goes tragically wrong); but a monk is no more than a Christian who has realized the full and stringent demands of his faith and whose life acts as an eschatological "sign" to the rest of the church. Pierre de Calan has something to say to those who live in "the world." To the religious vocation corresponds the vocation of marriage, which has the same criteria of fidelity and perseverance. After the publication of *Cosmas,* Calan was asked by a Christian group to write about fidelity in marriage. He explained the outline of his paper as follows: "All choice involves the risk of error. Everyone starts out in marriage with great love, but after a number of years the marriage can seem empty and vain. Fidelity alone can cope and compensate for the absence of the right dispositions—and it can sometimes create them." An austere doctrine, I remarked. "But," said he, "it is fundamentally Catholic."

1980

1

Cosmas's first cell was just here. He was baptized Jean and his surname came from an old Burgundy family of veterinary surgeons. No doubt it was this tradition that prompted him to take St. Cosmas as his patron when he began to serve God in the habit of the Reformed Cistercians. Cosmas was a doctor who emerged from Arabia with his brother Damien sometime toward the end of the third century. True, he was a doctor and not a vet. But when you are trying to heal and ease pain, it little matters whether it is men or animals who suffer . . .

Forgive me rambling on like this. We monks love the rule of silence: we love it because we need it. This holds for all the disciplines that we gladly accept when we come here: the strict timetable, the lack of freedom in the use of time, the uncomfortable broken sleep pattern, penances and fasting, work and prayer. All these are not self-inflicted punishments for their own sake—as some writers have suggested—nor are they a deliberate and masochistic attempt to win through to an antinatural mysticism.

The truth is much simpler, much more human. To welcome him who is the whole purpose of our lives, we do what the housewife instinctively does when she is expecting a guest: we tidy the place up, get rid of everything that is stained or dirty, make it spick-and-span. We know perfectly well that the complexes and obsessive neuroses by which some try to explain our lives on the human level really do exist in each one of us. And we know, too, that if we didn't master them by keeping a tight rein over our body and mind, our thoughts and actions, we would be overwhelmed by ourselves. We would no longer be open to the search for God that is at the heart of religious life. You wanted to see this for yourself for a few weeks. Quite naturally, the lover banishes from his thoughts everything that would distract him from the object of his love; quite naturally, he avoids the occasions that would place too great a strain on his fidelity. And that is what we do, quite naturally, when we obey our Rule.

Since Cosmas was here there have been some modifications in the harshness of our life, and some things have been made easier: the public confession of faults in the chapter has been abolished; presence at all the hours of the Divine Office is less strictly insisted upon; and some parts of the abbey, notably the church, are now heated during the winter. These changes formed part of an attempt to adapt to contemporary developments and ways of thinking. Perhaps more important, they express a desire to enhance our life of sacrifice, prayer, and work by stressing the spirit rather than the letter, free consent rather than external compulsion. Yet obedience remains as important as ever. It is a form of discipline that we cherish.

The rule of silence has also been modified. But most of us make only sparing use of the freedom we have been given. We know that silence provides the privileged way and the best environment for encountering God, growing in intimate union with Christ, and hearing the voice of the Spirit. We know, too, that silence fosters community life. Those who have never lived a monastic life might suppose that we are isolated and separated from one another because we speak only rarely. Nothing could be further from the truth. We are united in and by silence, like travelers sharing the same shelter or children crouching in the same hiding place. And we feel that the more we tried to communicate, the less we would commune.

Yet we remain human beings—and that was something that poor Cosmas found difficult to accept. Our need and love of silence do not prevent it being a burden, even after ten, twenty, or thirty years of monastic life. At the first opportunity a torrent of words will gush forth from us, rather like springs in mountain villages that overflow with joyous abundance. Our brother porters are famed for their garrulousness, and even they are outstripped by portresses in convents of women. You will discover that superiors like myself have the same temptation and are no better at resisting it.

This, then, was Cosmas's first cell. If you can call it a cell. This is where we sleep. The cells are no more than cubicles less than three yards long and two yards across, divided from one another by thin partitions that don't reach the ceiling. During sleep they are shut off by curtains made of rough, striped tent cloth, rather like the material used to cover a mattress.

When we are not sleeping the cubicles remain open. The visitor can see for himself the poverty of our common life. A simple wooden bed with a headpiece that takes the form of a child's crib—an unexpected tribute to elegance—a mattress and blankets beneath which we lie fully clothed. There is a crucifix on the wall, a clothes hook, a simple picture of Our Lady (a photograph of one of the innumerable statues carved by our Father Marie Bernard). There is no wardrobe, not even a box. The clothes we need are supplied by the brother in charge of the wardrobe. We have everything we need in the place where the Rule and the orders of our superiors prescribe that we will use it: so the psalter is in the church; books and periodicals are in the scriptorium, which is where we study; working clothes are in the changing room, where we leave our choir habits when we set off for the workshops or the farm; plates and cutlery are in the refectory. The monk not only has nothing of his own, he has nothing even entrusted to him. The only piece of furniture we have is a desk in the scriptorium.

All the cells look alike in their bareness and straight-line uniformity; if they did not have names inscribed above them, there would be no way of distinguishing between them. But after fifty years of religious life and having slept in a dozen or so different cells in this dormitory, I can assure you that most of them have some special feature. All the drafts from the staircase and corridor find their way into this cell, for instance. This one is always rather warm: even in the depths of winter it is the last to be reached by the rays of the setting sun, and it is assigned by custom to the oldest monk. When the moon comes up over the guesthouse, its first cold rays fall on the curtain of this cell. Here the partition unaccountably vibrates. And some cells have astonishing acoustic properties.

The directory of our order says that the monks of old used to consider the dormitory as an extension of the chapel. Compline, which we sing before going to bed, is the most restful of all our prayers. We offer to the Lord and lay before him the burden of the day that has just gone by. Like every other day, we have lived through it according to the prescriptions of our Rule. When Cosmas first came here, the timetable was very like the one you knew. We woke in the middle of the night, at three o'clock, for the office of Matins. We used to have prime and the chapter meeting. Then came a time for reading and private prayer, next the office of Lauds and the celebration of Mass. A couple of hours of manual work took us up to sext, just before lunch. Then in the afternoon, the same balanced life, governed by strict rules: the office of nones, then work on the farm or in the workshops, Vespers, a time for prayer, supper, another period for reading. When the Compline bell rings we come together in the church for the last time and peace descends, a reward for the austerity to which, throughout the long day, we have subjected our bodies and our minds.

You told me that you were very impressed by the solemn chant of the Salve Regina in the darkened church when only the statue of Our Lady, high above the choir, is illumined. What we are doing in fact is to entrust ourselves to the Mother of Peace for the coming night. Then we go to the dormitory in total silence and with souls gathered in complete peace and tranquility.

Usually a few noises will disturb this blessed calm. Familiar noises, almost liturgical in their predictability: Father Louis de Gonzague clearing his throat, Brother Jean de la Croix dropping his sandals on the floor, the two deep sighs that announce that Brother Paul Albert is dropping off to sleep. Monks usually sleep soundly. The limited time for sleep, the fatigue that comes from manual work, the tranquility of a life in which everything is foreseen, the deep inner peace that fills us—all these mean that once we lie down, we do not long remain awake, and insomnia is almost unknown. But it can sometimes happen that the abbey is disturbed by the noisy breathing of monks with flu or by the unconscious groanings of some of the brethren or by the creaking noise of the boards when an uneasy sleeper turns over. Every religious house knows the menace of snorers or that—fortunately less frequent—of monks who talk in their sleep.

Whenever possible the noisiest monks are given a dormitory of their own. And novices usually sleep apart, because we realize how difficult getting used to unwonted noises can be. When Cosmas came here, rebuilding work meant that only one common dormitory was available and he was assigned the noisiest of all the cells—a misfortune that was my fault.

Father Jacques Marie called it Denys's Ear. You have probably seen him and noticed his sharp features and hawklike look: he left my office just as you arrived. He's a former naval officer. He told us about the vast natural cavern at Syracuse in Sicily where prisoners were once kept. To please Denys the Tyrant, Archimedes had hollowed out a sort of tube halfway up the wall; and through it could be heard the slightest sigh, the most private whisper, and even the prisoners' breathing. In this way the tyrant could eavesdrop on confessions, plans for escape or flight, rumors of conspiracy. He was believed to be a magician.

Now Cosmas's first cell has the same odd acoustics. Whereas sounds reached most of the cubicles only after they had been muffled and hushed, Cosmas's cell was exceptionally noisy. He suffered a great deal from this, partly because he found it difficult to sleep, but even more, perhaps, because these sounds were for him a revelation of the minor defects and physical weaknesses of the monks. When he came to La Trappe his idealism made him imagine that we were disembodied spirits.

At that time I was what we call the novice master; that is, the monk who has charge of the novices' formation. During my time in the abbey I had twice lived in that cell and knew what it was like. I ought to have realized that Cosmas, with his extreme sensitivity and his unrealistic vision of monks and monastic life, would be disturbed by this excessive noise. Perhaps a quieter cell would not have enabled him to avoid the first breakdown, but it was certainly made worse by a lack of sleep. It was a bad blunder to put this sensitive novice, who depended so much on his environment, into Denys's Ear. I was fully responsible for the decision and take the blame.

2

Now here is Cosmas's last resting place: the small rectangle of consecrated ground where all that remains of his mortal flesh mingles with the clay of the earth.

You know that monks are buried without a coffin, on the clay, just like that, in their choir habit. Their bodily remains are unprotected against water, worms, underground rodents, and the infinitely small creatures that quickly turn into humus whatever is buried in the soil. Some people are horrified at the thought of this return to the earth by way of gradual decomposition. We think of it as normal. At funerals we pay respect to the body because it has been the dwelling place of the soul and the instrument of a human will. But we know that our earthly husk has fulfilled its task by the time we come to die. Why should we delay our return to dust by means of a few planks coated with zinc or lead? There is a strength and an ordered beauty in natural processes: it is good that matter should return to matter. The cross on which the name of each monk is inscribed is not put there to stand guard over a body that is of no more use to him; it hints at the truth that the dead live forever only in virtue of our redemption.

Toward dusk on a gray day like today you can hardly see our cemetery. You need to be up at dawn on a clear day when the rising sun bathes the apse and the side chapels with burnished mauve, and prolongs the shadow of the crosses on the brown earth still dank with dew. One understands why the Germans call a cemetery a *Friedhof*, a field of peace.

Our graves are as identical as our cells. Just a slightly raised mound of earth beneath a cross that bears the name the monk had in religion: here Brother Clement, there Father Bonaventure. A monk does not break all the bonds of love when he enters La Trappe: all his life long, he will remain a son, a brother, an uncle, a cousin, an affectionate friend. But henceforward, his real family is the Cistercian family. Anonymity makes each one of us a stone in the building, a handful of flour in the dough . . . Under the dead monk's name, his status in religious life: priest, lay brother, novice, oblate. And then a single date: the date of death, which is for us the moment of being born to real life.

As you can see the cross that marks the place where Cosmas is buried is rather vague: *February 1938*. We never knew the exact day of his death. Above the date: *Brother Cosmas, novice.* At that time some thought the inscription went too far: strictly speaking, Cosmas was not a member of the community when his corpse was discovered.

Father Abbot had at first obtained permission to have Cosmas buried in the parish cemetery: this was a provisional arrangement, so long as his family did not ask for his mortal remains. His body had been moved into the abbey church for the vigil. He was to be placed in his coffin next morning, the coffin having been hastily ordered from Brother Paul, the joiner. Six monks were appointed to accompany the body to the parish church of Soligny, where they would sing the Office of the Dead before the funeral.

We took it in turns, two by two, to watch over him throughout the night. The candles cast a hesitant light on the body, which lay on a trestle table covered with a black cloth. Specks of gold flickered on the brass candlesticks of the altar. As the wind caught the candles, the seat rests in the nearest choir stalls gleamed briefly. A shifting frontier of shadow enfolded this pool of light, merging into total darkness toward the end of the nave, behind the altar, and in the arms of the transept. It was a starless, moonless night toward the end of winter, damp and cold, and one could scarcely make out the frame of the stained-glass windows.

Between the recitation of the psalms there were long pauses for silent prayer. It must have been about midnight, the time when Father Emmanuel and I were due to be replaced and to return to the dormitory. I was asking God to welcome our deceased brother and, in his mercy, to make allowances for all his sufferings and disappointments—especially for the dream-vision of religious life, pursued since childhood, which Cosmas could neither abandon nor realize.

I could almost see him in the same church, right at the start of his novitiate, keeping watch over the body of Father Élie, whose face had taken on a waxlike transparency and whose forehead, in the candlelight, gleamed like old ivory. Something prompted me to turn and observe Cosmas: his gaze seemed to be riveted on the face of the dead monk, and his expression was a strange mixture of fascination and contentment. I noticed the same expression when the body of Father Élie was placed in his grave and gradually buried. Cosmas seemed to fear neither death nor burial. That same evening he said to me:

"What a grace it is, Father, to think that my body will be buried like that."

Was this perhaps the memory that came back to me at that precise moment? Or was it a deeper inspiration? . . .

The presence of the Holy Spirit is such a living reality for us and it lingers within the walls of the abbey so much that our first thought is to attribute to him any idea that occurs to us. But while our life of penance and prayer and the intimacy that we strive for in our relationship with the three persons of the Trinity make us tend to detect the influence of the Spirit in the workings of our minds, humility and the wisdom of experience prevent us from attributing to him our every whim. My imagination could have been overstimulated through lack of sleep, the deep upset caused by the death of Cosmas and the tragic circumstances of his discovery, and by the strain of a prayer in which I was desperately trying to commune with the soul of Cosmas, now in the hands of God.

The brothers who were to take over from us came into the church. When I got back to the dormitory and had drawn the curtain of my cell, I was afraid I might be unable to sleep. In fact I fell immediately into a deep and peaceful sleep for the short period that remained to me.

A few hours later, after Matins in the middle of the night, I met Father Abbot just outside the cloister, which is for us, as the Rule splendidly says, "the workshop of the spiritual life." I bowed low before him and said "Benedicte." He looked at me for a moment before answering, "Dominus."

"Reverend Father," I said, "an idea has been on my mind throughout the night."

He looked at me again for some time, as was his custom. My predecessor, Dom Philippe Jalluy, was tall, austere, and intimidating. He had the drawn features and the slim, tall appearance that I lack and that people instinctively expect to find in a monk, especially in an abbot. When he turned his head, his shoulders moved as well: although this seemed to us to manifest his concern for dignity, it was in fact due to a spinal defect. His face was one of the most motionless I have ever known, and only his eyelids seemed to move, ever so slowly, and the movement of the eyes was slower still. It was only toward the end of his life that we finally grasped that he had undergone great suffering, and that his impassivity was the mask of heroism. Simply by seeing him kneeling at the altar, most of the monks were persuaded that he enjoyed mystical experiences. We felt guided by him, caught up in the perfection that the Rule enjoins. But it took courage to approach him: he was an awesome figure, and he did not exactly inspire plain speaking.

Was it perhaps true that over and above his physical suffering, he had also had to undergo deep spiritual trials? Some of the greatest monks have known fearful difficulties and almost unbearable doubts concerning faith or hope. Dom Philippe never confided in any of us, except perhaps in Father Laurent, who was his confessor. He was one of those heroic souls who have not the slightest trace of self-pity and who put into practice the tough maxim of Clotilde de Vaux: "It is unworthy of heroic souls to spread abroad the distress they feel."

On his father's side he came from a rich and traditionally Jansenist family of Lyons. His Parisian mother had a very liberal background, and there were writers and musicians in the family. The sensitivity that came from his mother undoubtedly made the lack of human love in religious life a cause of suffering. But he had opted once and for all for his father's austerity. To seek to please would have seemed to him cowardice. The way he announced his decisions—and they were usually right—was disconcerting: he never felt he had to give the reasons for them. Though his psychological grasp could be penetrating, his temperament inclined him to rapid black-and-white judgments. Not that he ever lost his temper, unlike some of the most famous Cistercian abbots. But the curtness and—often—the irony of his remarks kept us at a distance, "at barge-pole length," said Father Jacques Marie.

Death alone seemed to release him from his sense of being the abbot and to allow him to become a father and a friend, for in death the soul of the deceased monk passed out of his hands and was entrusted to the judgment of God. More than once at the deathbed of one of the monks I saw him shed tears, reveal his humanity, or say a few words of infinite gentleness.

He had a splendid singing voice, and his questions rang out like assertions. And so on that morning, when he had surveyed me with his pale blue eyes, he asked, "It's about Cosmas?" I knew that I had no need to answer.

Dom Philippe led me to his office and nodded for me to sit down and then to speak. He paced up and down in silence while I told him about my feeling, my conviction that the mortal remains of Cosmas should be buried not in the parish graveyard at Soligny but in the monastic cemetery, next to the church and alongside Brother Thaddée, whom we had buried just a few days before.

Dom Philippe seemed taken aback by this suggestion. After a pause he pointed out that our cemetery was part of the monastic enclosure: it was open only to monks or oblates or very close friends whose lives had been entirely devoted to the community or who had shared in its atmosphere. Cosmas had died almost two years after leaving the abbey, to which he had never returned, and therefore he could not in the ordinary way take his place among the monks. Then he said:

"If you really want it, Father, we could treat him as a friend of the abbey, although . . ."

It often happened that Dom Philippe left his sentences trailing in the air, and this gave an added sense of remoteness to what he said.

I waited for a moment, just to make sure that Dom Philippe had nothing more to add. Then I explained that what I had in mind went further than what he was suggesting. I did not want Cosmas to be buried in the monastic cemetery as a friend, but as a member of the community, as the novice that he intended to be once more when death had taken him away from us. Had we not given him permission to return and to have one last chance of trying to fulfill what he believed to be his vocation? If he had not mysteriously died on the way to La Trappe, if he had once more put on the novice's habit, and if he had died only a few days later, then we would have buried him among the monks. Was it altogether fair that death should have prevented him from realizing our agreement?

Father Abbot smiled vaguely as he interrupted me:

"Why do you speak of *our* agreement? You have a short memory, Father. You presented me with a fait accompli, and as you will remember, all I said was, 'Let God's grace take its course.' . . ."

I accepted this. It was perfectly true that after a conversation with his friend, Dominique, I had agreed without consulting anyone else that Cosmas should return. Father Abbot went on:

"Let's not go back over the past. Your question is perfectly straightforward. Ought we now to treat Cosmas as though he were a member of the community? This was his intention, and you had given your approval . . ."

After a pause for thought he said:

"This boy, you know, has always been something of a mystery for us. I would like to discuss the matter with the council."

If I did not mistrust the military metaphors that have abounded in spiritual literature for so long, I would describe the abbot's council as a sort of general staff—or, if you prefer a civilian comparison, a board of management. Nowadays one or two members are elected as representatives of the whole community. At that time they were all appointed by Father Abbot. They included the prior and the subprior; the cellarer and the secretary, who were in charge of the material life of the abbey; and sometimes one or two monks whose judgment the abbot trusted. I was a member as novice master.

Father Abbot summoned us just before the office of prime.

All the details of the scene come back to me with astonishing clarity. Father Abbot asked me to sit down by his desk, while the other members of the council sat opposite in a semicircle. Surveying the group, I marveled once again at the effects of religious life. Just like brothers and sisters, and despite obvious differences in appearance, members of the same religious order come to have a family likeness. It is not explained simply by their dress or attitudes. It has a deeper cause: it expresses the inner illumination that comes from a life of prayer. But far from stifling personality and making everyone look the same, this family likeness enhances the difference. One thinks of paintings by old masters where the uniformity of dress heightens the diversity of faces and character.

Father Léon, the prior, was at that time the only choir monk who wore a beard—a broad, white, fanlike beard. He reminded me of St. Peter, but of St. Peter in old age when he had mellowed and was writing those letters that are so full of gentleness. The subprior, Father Athanase, was a very different character: he was much younger, had rather a stiff military bearing, and was later deported to Germany for his active involvement in the resistance. There he died. The appearance of the cellarer and the secretary matched the work they did. Father Cellarer had the jovial and energetic look of a commercial traveler or small businessman. Although Father Secretary had been a carpenter before entering religious life, in his steel-rimmed spectacles he looked the perfect administrator. Nearest to me, finally, were the two wise men appointed by the abbot, although they had no official position: the enigmatic and highly intelligent Father Marie Silvestre, and dear Father Emmanuel, with the profile of a stained-glass saint and a look of great gentleness—of all my brothers in religion he was the one closest to my heart.

Father Abbot asked me briefly to run through the argument I had put to him an hour ago. My proposal seemed to be greeted with a combination of indifference, surprise, and weariness. Cosmas had been the unwitting cause of a lot of trouble. The great charity of the men gathered around Dom Philippe did not stop them thinking that the time had come, now that Cosmas was at rest, for them to share in his repose. Father Subprior repeated the objections of principle that the abbot had at first put to me. Father Secretary pointed out that if Cosmas were to be buried without a coffin, like a monk, it would be difficult to return the body to his family later, should they request it. The other members of the council indicated by a gesture or their silence that the whole matter seemed trivial, that my suggestion failed to arouse their enthusiasm, and that they would abide by the decision of Father Abbot. Father Emmanuel was the only one to use the word *compassion:* he looked at me briefly, and I understood that he was thinking of me as much and perhaps rather more than of Cosmas.

Dom Philippe pondered this for a moment, slowly turned toward Father Emmanuel, and then said:

"You are right. Cosmas will be buried this evening in the community cemetery. We will say the Office of the Dead immediately after nones."

Then he turned toward me:

"Father, you will cancel the ceremony arranged for tomorrow and offer my apologies to the parish priest of Soligny. And you will ask Brother Gabriel to clothe the body in a novice's habit."

Father Abbot's decision took everyone, including myself, by surprise; I had not dared hope for it; the others expected him to give reasons for this waiving of our customs. But as usual he did not explain his decision. The council was at an end.

After prime, Father Abbot informed the chapter of the arrangements for Cosmas's funeral, still without justifying his decision. The sense of surprise and the need for some explanation were just as strong as they had been in the council. But none of the monks dared to question Dom Philippe.

And monks are so inclined and trained to obedience that the funeral service and the burial took place not superficially but sincerely, as though we were burying and commending to God the oldest member of the community.

According to custom the body had been washed and clothed, as Father Abbot had prescribed, in a novice's habit, with the hood drawn down over the face to conceal the marks made by the animal bites. When Dom Philippe cast the first spadeful of earth on the body, and when the bearers filled in the grave, the devout calm on all sides made it clear that we were indeed burying our brother Cosmas, novice, by the apse of our church, beneath the wooden cross, and under the barely perceptible mound of earth.

Great joy and gratitude came over me. I could hardly put it into words, but in the depths of my being I felt, gently and ceaselessly, an invasion of light. At that moment it seemed as though the clouds that had darkened Cosmas's life were now dissipated, and that joy and order once more prevailed. As for the reasons that had led Father Abbot to accede to my last request on behalf of Cosmas, I only understood them, in all their depth and richness, many months later when Dom Philippe and I had a conversation beside de Rancé Lake.

3

But was Cosmas really called to religious life? No other question has ever disturbed me so much.

A vocation is not open to empirical investigation. The Lord is relentless when he wants to enlist someone in his service; but he is also incredibly self-effacing. One cannot possibly understand the signs of a vocation unless one remembers that God, because he is love, woos souls with all the delicacy and shyness of a lover. Even those who, like myself, can say that they have never had the slightest doubt about their vocation, still feel overwhelmed and at a loss to explain exactly what this means. For here contradictory truths, inaccessible to ordinary human logic, come together: there is a sense of being led by someone stronger than oneself, and yet of remaining free; the feeling that the voice that calls us will never fall silent, that it will pursue us in season and out of season, and yet that it is within our power at any given moment not to heed it; the understanding that God has need of our cooperation to lead us wherever he desires. Mary was free to say no to the angel.

Moreover, God's call comes to us in a human context that may be ambivalent and need sorting out: family circumstances; the influence of a priest or of relations or friends; an example one feels impelled to follow; a book we have read, or a feeling; psychological or emotional events. All these can be exploited by the Lord to incline us to follow his path. But they may also lead to fantasy vocations or down blind alleys.

There are so many different ways of serving God. Someone who thought he was made for a contemplative vocation realizes that the active life is the right way for him. The outsider may think that the different branches within the same religious family are of no consequence. Yet they express the following truth of experience: religious life is a delicate balance in which health, cast of mind, and spiritual dispositions all play their part. One of my young cousins tried three different religious congregations, with the result that her family no longer took her vocation seriously; but her perseverance led her in the end into the community for which, all along and without realizing it, she had been destined. She has now lived there for twenty years in complete harmony with herself and—so it seems—with God.

What else can I say to show how carefully an inner call must be scrutinized?

That a man's spiritual destiny may develop or come to maturity late. I have in mind not simply late vocations that bring to us men who want to dedicate the rest of their years to God, often after they have been widowed. There are many diocesan priests who first give themselves heart and soul to parish work before coming here in search of peace but also of an alternative form of apostolate. It often happens that a youthful vocation, abandoned because one could not be sure about it, is reanimated and fulfilled twenty years later.

Outside circumstances may change the nature of the call for those whom the Lord summons to his service. A war, for instance, may make the contemplative life more desirable, and the spectacle of human stupidity, devastation, and violence can make the silence and calm of a consecrated life more attractive.

It is a difficult and sometimes awesome task to distinguish between truth and error, to determine whether a vocation is genuine or illusory. A heavy burden of responsibility rests on parents who put pressure on their children, on religious superiors or seminary rectors who are too self-assured and do not have enough respect for individual psychology and the action of grace; they can easily become obstacles to the realization of a genuine vocation. A similar burden of responsibility falls on those who fail to detect, as soon as possible, a nonvocation.

In a religious community like ours, it is the abbot, aided by his council, who accepts or rejects postulants for the novitiate.

During the period of formation he has to decide whether the man has what it takes to be a monk. But though the ultimate decision belongs to Father Abbot, the task of discernment before and after entry into the novitiate rests upon the individual himself with the help and guidance of the novice master.

The best advice one can give to someone who believes he is made for monastic life is that he should think it over in an atmosphere of simplicity of heart, without getting either excited or tense, and that he should pray with confidence.

Those entrusted with the task of guiding others, young or old, who feel called by the Lord, must be both prudent and humble. If all spiritual fathers had as much respect for their charges as God has for each one of us, there would be fewer tragic errors in the direction of souls.

Our first duty is to remember that we are human. We must, of course, beg for help from on high in the discharge of our responsibility toward the novices. But we have also to steer clear of all illuminism that would leave us waiting for God to tell us what to do. The Holy Spirit can counsel us, in the manner and to the extent that are appropriate to him. Sometimes he enlightens our minds in a most wonderful way. But he never deprives us of our responsibility. If he is not to botch his work, the novice master must have sterling qualities of equanimity, balanced judgment, common sense, and a grasp of psychology. If a monk like myself were allowed to give his own opinion on the reasons why his superiors entrusted him with this office, I would put it down to the placidity that I owe to my father and the lack of romanticism that so disappointed Cosmas.

In the eight years in which I had to diagnose the genuineness of several dozen vocations, I always tried to set aside snap judgments and immediate feelings and confined myself to the three criteria by which the authenticity of a vocation can be recognized. First the fact that someone feels drawn to the monastic life. Then his aptitude for it: it is not enough simply to want to be an airline pilot, you also need good eyesight, quick reflexes, and considerable cool—and neither is the desire to be a monk enough unless one has or has acquired the right frame of mind, the ability to adapt to community life, a certain physical and mental toughness, and the right spiritual dispositions. And finally one needs grace, which can take many different forms.

To call those who do not hear his voice clearly enough, God sometimes uses an illness, an accident, some misfortune or other, very rarely a vision. You know perhaps that God had to jolt St. Teresa of Ávila several times before she became a saint.

On the other hand, I was recently told the story of a very generous young woman who embarked on a mistaken vocation after some emotional disappointments. She was persuaded that her desire to serve God could be realized only through the most rigorous separation from the world, and was encouraged in this belief by a rather overenthusiastic confessor; and so she chose a cloistered and contemplative order. She had only been there a year when the pain began. It was an odd form of pain: whenever the young nun went into choir and began to pray, she felt a pressure between the shoulder blades, as though a weight were pressing down against the spine. The community doctor found this beyond his competence. The superior, who supposed it must be due to some nervous trouble, sent her away to spend a few weeks with her family. The pain disappeared immediately, but when the time came for her to return to the community, it was obvious that nothing had changed . . .

I will spare you the details of the psychological martyrdom she must have gone through, the alternating bouts of hope and disappointment that lasted for two years. She went from clinic to clinic, hospital to hospital, throughout the world. She tried every form of treatment and put herself in the hands of the finest specialists and—in all probability—the worst charlatans. Finally she agreed to go to a sort of Indian guru. He was perhaps the most honest and clear-sighted of all those who had examined her. He said: "Mademoiselle, you are a Christian. This is a matter for your God or your evil spirits. No man can do anything for you, and I can do no more and no less than anyone else."

She made a pilgrimage to Lourdes. She persuaded someone to exorcise her. When she left the convent, the pain soon became less frequent and then disappeared altogether. She imagined she was cured. But as soon as she was back in the community—or at least as soon as she kneeled down before the tabernacle for the first time—the suffering returned, unbearably.

She was forced to admit that she should now give up what she had believed, and was still tempted to believe, was her vocation. With sadness in her heart, she went back to the lay state and resumed the study of biology that she had started before entering the convent. She became assistant to a research worker about ten years older than herself. Through their work together they one day became aware that they wanted to share their entire life. The mysterious pain that had prevented her from following her vocation never returned; she now has four children and thanks God daily for letting her understand that she was on the wrong path.

But why did he do it in such a surprising and indeed cruel way? Instead of baffling pain, why couldn't God have granted this girl the grace of lucidity about herself? Questions like these go beyond human understanding, and the answers do not belong to this world. Are the trials undergone by this unfortunate girl more upsetting for human reason than the folly of the cross? And yet the God who in his Son has borne this suffering for our salvation must surely be free to make demands on us, as he sees fit, if only to remind us that he is the master.

But usually the action of grace takes less tragic and more human forms. A book happens to come your way that throws light on monastic life—and you feel repelled or attracted. Or it may be a conversation. Or a pilgrimage. Or the winding up of a family responsibility—sick or impoverished parents to be cared for, younger brothers or sisters to be brought up—that made it impossible even to think of entering religious life. Perhaps you would want to call chance what I am calling grace. But for a Christian—remember the dying words Bernanos attributes to his country priest—everything is grace, chance included.

It would be pretentious, ridiculous, and simply wrong for me to say that these three criteria—attraction, aptitude, grace—applied in a context of humble prayer, and only after observing and listening to the novices and postulants entrusted to me and helping them to reflect on themselves in peace and objectivity, enabled me to make no mistakes. Even so, whenever I had to advise Father Abbot on the acceptance or rejection of a candidate, I think I may say in all humility that I have always known, with reasonable speed and certainty, what the decision should be.

Except in one case: that of Cosmas.

Cosmas was certainly drawn to religious life. He always maintained that he felt drawn to it in the clearest and most imperious possible manner.

I would be inclined to say, moreover, that he had every aptitude needed for religious life, except one—but it is an aptitude
of immense importance: the ability to accept human realities.
During the months he spent at La Trappe the ease and thor-
oughness with which he adapted to our way of life and prayer
led me to think that he was a born monk. But his successive
departures—and the second time he practically fled—seemed
to point to the conclusion that he was not made for religious
life at all.

As for grace, I wondered for a long time how the signs
should be interpreted. Were the trials that the Lord sent him in
abundance an indication that he was on the wrong path? His
resolution in opposing first the judgment of Father Abbot and
then mine, which made no sense in human terms, could not be
based, in my knowledge of him, on mere pride and stubbornness: ought we therefore to interpret it as a supernatural inspiration? And what meaning were we to give to his death, which
came tragically and mysteriously when he was on the point of
returning to us? Was it the Lord's final refusal to allow Cosmas
to enter La Trappe—or was it rather the providential solution
to a vocation that was genuine enough but that, by a mysterious
decree of the divine will, was never to be realized?

4

Dominique, who was doing a practical course here, took this photograph of Cosmas in the summer after he first came back.

The tradition is that the Trappist farm should be a model for others. This is partly because we want to do well what we have to do, but also to improve the methods of agriculture and livestock breeding in an area that has so far been somewhat backward. I remember how surprised and scandalized Cosmas was when he discovered that we entered our bulls and milk cows for agricultural competitions—and hoped that they would win. In the first period of his noviceship he found this concern for earthly rewards rather disconcerting.

Our farming exploits mean that almost every summer we take on a few students from agricultural colleges: they come for five or six weeks in the middle of their two-year course. Their knowledge of farming is rather bookish, but the extra manpower is useful to us in the high season. They bring a breath of the outside world, and whatever their personal convictions they show a great deal of respect for monastic discipline and the rule of silence. Most of them, even those of no faith, become aware—as you yourself did—of the fascination of religious life. Occasionally one or other of them begins to wonder vaguely whether he has not the first stirrings of a vocation. They usually do no more than toy with the idea briefly, only to laugh about it a few days later. There was one who came back never more to leave: Brother Augustin, who has run the farm for years and who is easily recognized by his baldness and his immense height. He has been completely bald ever since I've known him.

Dominique was the only student doing a course with us that year. He came from the Midi and had found his way to the hills of Le Perche for no fathomable reason. As it happened the summer was fine and the sun matched Dominique's southern accent. As the son of a university teacher and someone who had been brought up in a rationalistic environment, he affected to be totally free from any metaphysical anxiety; yet it was obvious that he was fascinated by our lifestyle. His hair was black and his skin dark. He had the sharp, darting eyes of a squirrel. He was short and slim but good with his hands and had astonishing nervous energy. Even in repose or sitting down, he was forever moving a foot or a leg or an arm. He was a nonstop talker. He was rather like one of those women who can never go about their work in silence: he needed a background of words in order to do anything. But he never waited for an answer.

We were just finishing building a silo tower to contain green fodder sprayed by lactic acids: if you have ever passed that way when the daily ration for the animals is being prepared, you will not be able to forget the characteristic smell. Father Cellarer was a very able administrator, but he suffered—and he made us suffer—from an appalling lack of taste. The silo was built in cheap neo-Gothic. The abbey buildings, as you have seen for yourself, are devoid of architectural interest. The original guesthouse, which now houses the flour mill and the grain supplies, has all the charm of the oldest buildings of Le Perche: it is built out of rough-hewn flint stone, cemented by the yellow sand from the neighboring quarries, and its steeply pitched roof is of uneven brown tiles. It dates from the thirteenth century. What used to be the abbot's lodgings, built by the Abbé de Rancé, the reformer of La Trappe and friend of Bossuet and Saint-Simon—who at that time held court at Ferté-Vidame, his Normandy version of Versailles—dates from about 1680. As you have seen it is well proportioned and has a certain grandeur. Everything else was rebuilt toward the end of the nineteenth century in a somewhat ill-defined style in which pseudo-Gothic prevails but that also includes barrel vaults and barracks-like windows. But that did not justify the bizarre building we had to put up that summer, a silo masquerading as a medieval tower. From every point of view it is a disgrace to the abbey. From your guest room you are probably spared the sight of its battlements, its grain elevator that looks like a gallows, its watchtower for an imaginary guard—all made of concrete blocks. In the photograph Cosmas is standing in line and handing a block to a lay brother.

Dominique had a rather mocking affection for Cosmas. He bullied him to say whether he should be called by his baptismal name, Jean, or his religious name, Cosmas, though he still had not taken his vows; so Dominique called him now Jean-Cosmas, now Cosmas-Jean, lengthening the *o* in either case.

His great sport was to ask point-blank questions in order to get Cosmas to break silence other than was needed for the work in hand. Or he would pretend to be talking to himself, and in a voice loud enough to be heard by Cosmas would denounce his alleged ambition: "Cosmas-Jean, Cosmas-Jean, you are a climber, a climber of holiness. You are much too keen. You think you're God's favorite."

Or: "My dear brother Jean-Cosmas, I know you are a candidate for canonization long before your death. You're not even a Trappist novice: you are an archangel novice."

However, I think that Dominique had already perfectly well grasped the nature of Cosmas's difficulties, and that his teasing was a way of helping him to find the right balance. I am quite sure that he was fond of him. He was to prove it more than abundantly later on.

I had the photograph enlarged. Its aesthetic value is slight, but it remains the best likeness we have of Cosmas.

The most striking feature is the height and width of the brow, which seemed to be out of proportion with the rest of his face: it was as though he had borrowed it from another head, as one replaces a piece of outworn equipment. This lack of proportion made him seem on the small side: in fact he was of average height and was well built, though he had a slight stoop. You will also notice the rather short, pointed nose in a face that is on the whole round, the thick lips—sign of goodness—the firm, sturdy chin, the bushy eyebrows that indicate stubbornness. But what one misses in this photograph is the look of his brown-green eyes, a gentle but often impenetrable look in which acute perception could easily give way to surprised naïveté, and that combined uneasiness and trust, gaiety, and sometimes a world-weary sadness.

I wasn't completely at ease with him during our first meetings. The look we exchange with someone is already a language of confidence, friendship, and love; and that is even truer in a monastery. People have fixed in their minds the image of *Sombres Trappes*—that was the title of a book published by the Abbey of St. Wandrille some thirty years ago—and think of gloomy places where the monks, confined in their hoods like horses in their blinkers, live alongside one another in mutual ignorance, their gaze fixed on the ground when it is not directed to the altar or the psalter, immured in themselves as much as within the walls of the abbey.

Nothing could be further from the truth. It may be true that we are rather reserved toward one another—that is an aspect of silence—and that we do not watch one another with the insistent curiosity of people in the world. But if the looks we exchange are deliberately brief and controlled, they are also frank, contented, and uninhibited. Spiritual affection is charged with the affection of Christ as it is seen throughout the Gospels—in his attitude toward children, his disciples, and the women in need of forgiveness. When the eyes of two monks meet, they have nothing to hide from each other, for they know that they are engaged upon a quest for a love and a truth that transcend them both. They can meet in an instant and say what lengthy speeches could never express: that each of them recognizes in the other that transparent joy that he himself feels.

At my first meeting with Cosmas there was a rather surprising contrast between his general demeanor and the look in his eyes. He talked easily—with the slight slurring accent of Burgundy—and even abundantly, and yet very simply and without any false note, concerned only to say precisely what he had to say. He was a good listener, too, so long as his keenness to make a point clear did not lead him to interrupt. His whole concern was to communicate and make contact. And yet the look in his eyes seemed to disclose something else, a different, shifting, and elusive reality that he probably could not control and that lurked somewhere behind the feelings and the thoughts that he articulated.

In someone other than Cosmas one might have concluded that this contrast among attitudes, language, and look was evidence of a tendency to duplicity, or at least to concealment. But when one came to know him better, this idea seemed not merely unjust: it was absurd. I understood it only gradually: whenever there was this contrast between the look of Cosmas and what he said and did, one knew that a crisis was brewing, just as a troubled sky announces the coming storm.

5

Our first conversation left me with the feeling that here was a classic case of a vocation.

I was in my office when there was a knock at the door. One of the brothers who worked in the guesthouse bowed low, withdrew, and left Cosmas standing there in the doorway. I invited him to come in and sit down. With his back to the glass panel of the door—the only source of light—I could see him in silhouette. I noticed already his distinctive features—the broad, high forehead, the short nose, the square chin; but I couldn't really make out the finer aspects of his look and expression. At first glance I would have said that he was twenty-two or twenty-three: in fact he was just nineteen.

We are quite used to visitors like him: young men or men not so young who come and stay in the guesthouse, take part in most of the Divine Office, and go for endless walks in the woods and round the lake. We sense that they are praying and meditating with great intensity, but we are even more aware that they are scrutinizing us keenly and trying to get to know every detail of our life. The end of the story is nearly always the same: one day, usually on the eve of their presumed departure, as though they were afraid to break the spell by revealing their plans too soon, they ask Father Guest Master for permission to speak to the abbot or the monk in charge of vocations.

Cosmas was no exception to the rule: he had been staying for ten days in the guesthouse and—so the guest master informed me—had to leave by the end of the week at the latest . . . I asked him to tell me his story.

He explained that six years earlier he had come to La Trappe to make a retreat with a group of boys from his college. These few days lived alongside the community had left him unforgettable memories: the hooded yet animated outline of the monks at prayer in the choir, celebrating the praise of God with the tranquil simplicity of Gregorian chant; the looming shapes moving meditatively around the cloister; the slow procession of monks on their way to the refectory or the chapter room; the teams of monks setting off in silence for their work, now indistinguishable in their working garb. The choir monks had removed their white cowls and the lay brothers their brown habits: since then the distinctions between the two sorts of monk have been abolished.

A longing for this peaceful, harmonious life had never left him. He felt nostalgic for the beauty of our landscapes, and for the order of a life governed by bells that seemed to express an invitation, an accompaniment, and a consecration to the service of God. When he left school he started on a science degree to please his parents and to prepare himself vaguely for the entrance examination to the veterinary college at Maisons-Alfort. But his heart wasn't in it. After an exam failure that he admitted to having half desired, his vocation seemed to be ever more secure. He had come here two months before, but then a shyness that he could no longer understand had stopped him from revealing his vocation. So he had come back for a second visit, which was concluded that evening in my office.

The bell was ringing for choir. I arranged to see Cosmas the next day after nones, which followed the midday meal. I asked him to wait for me in his room in the guesthouse. I preferred to see him in a different setting, better lit than my office, and where he would feel less intimidated.

He greeted me with the confident and discreet smile that was part of his charm. I sat down on the only available chair, while he sat on the edge of the bed with his rather short legs dangling down, his hands on the blanket as he leaned forward, his face catching the light. I watched him carefully for the two hours I was with him, noting his attitudes, his way of speaking and listening, his varied expressions. I became aware of something I had not noticed the day before: a combination of good-will and attentiveness together with a certain obstinacy that came out in the way he kept on repeating the same phrases; the eyes that I had thought were brown were less dark and seemed almost to verge on green; but most of all the discrepancy between the calm assurance of what he was saying and the furtive anxiety that could be read in his eyes.

At the start of our second meeting I tried to get things sorted out: everything he had said the previous day about the fascination of our Trappist life was very gratifying but it was also very superficial and belonged to—dare I say it?—folklore. I wanted him to tell me the deeper reasons that had led him to want to enter religious life, and why he had chosen the Benedictine family and, within it, this particular branch of Reformed Cistercians. He admitted that his choice of La Trappe owed a good deal to chance and to the fact that he had made a retreat here with a dozen or so of his fellow pupils under the guidance of an elderly priest who was chaplain to his class. He asked, naively and rather anxiously, whether in my view such an accidental choice was a negative sign. I said that was obviously not so, but that he would have to ratify the choice when he had a better grasp of his motives.

The reasons he gave for his religious vocation belong to a realm in which all discussion is awkward: it was based on inner certainty that he did not appear to have sifted critically. For Cosmas it was self-evident that he was called to the exclusive service of the Lord and equally self-evident that the life of a secular priest would not suit him. I tried several times to get him to tell me the precise form that this inner call took, whether he had felt it continually since he first came here or only spasmodically, and what doubts and hesitations he had experienced. He tried hard to answer my questions simply and directly, but it was obvious that he found them rather odd. No, he had never had any doubts: and it was only out of obedience to his parents that he had continued his studies before asking to be admitted to La Trappe. He gave me the name of a priest with whom he had discussed his plans and of the few friends he had informed: I was surprised to find that he did not mention any member of his family.

He dwelled most convincingly and at the greatest length on his desire for a Benedictine community. He knew the Rule of St. Benedict almost by heart, and seemed happy at the idea of a strictly ordered life in the service of the only Being who deserved a total dedication of body and soul. Should I have noticed there and then (but such details only strike one later, when things have taken their course, and maybe one really imagines them owing to the almost inescapable need to explain everything with hindsight), should I have noticed that he spoke far too exclusively of the Divine Office, of prayer and penance, and not enough about the actual work of a monk? I didn't realize how seraphic and out of this world were his ideas on community life, even though he could describe it with remarkable precision as though he had already lived it himself.

By the end of the interview I felt rather embarrassed. Cosmas had presented me with one of those vocations that, at first sight, one has no grounds for discouraging. It was like a smooth mountain face, with neither cracks nor crevices that one could hold on to; and yet in his ascent he would need them to appreciate the obstacles and difficulties that he would inevitably have to face as a future novice.

His resolve seemed to be too perfect and too straightforward, and the unprecedented absence of problems and inner tensions made me think that although Cosmas's vocation was serious enough, it would need time to come to full maturity. I advised him to test it out for another year while he continued with his secular studies. As he had already passed his baccalaureate in mathematics, I suggested a year of philosophy. I also advised him to develop his knowledge of Scripture and of the doctrine of the church, which seemed to me to be still only up to the standard of a good student rather than of someone who had really strengthened his faith by study and reflection. Besides the directory and customs book of our order, I recommended a list of books that he could usefully read and promised to send him a further list later. In the course of this year, he could come whenever he liked, stay in the guesthouse, and at the very least he should make a fifteen-day retreat in the spring. Then, if the divine call still seemed clear to him, and if we could discover no objections, he would begin his military service; and if he emerged unshaken from that experience, his application to the noviceship would be officially submitted to Father Abbot and presented to the community.

He listened patiently to my advice and accepted my suggestions as though they were perfectly obvious.

The way he carried out this program confirmed him in the certainty that he was called to religious life and me in the conviction that I had no reason to discourage him. With his permission I had written to several priests who had known him and to some of his former teachers. They all agreed that Cosmas had always been deeply religious both as a child and a young man; no adolescent crisis had disturbed the clarity of his vision or the purity of his conduct; the community that accepted him would be most certainly enriched by his presence.

In the first year he spent a few days at La Trappe in Advent, at the beginning of Lent, and, as suggested, two weeks around Whitsunday. During these visits I saw him frequently and at some length.

I tried to help him to understand monastic spirituality and the dispositions that are needed in the service of the Lord. Although he listened very attentively, I seemed to be telling him what he already knew. And that was probably why I didn't stress as much as I should the more humble and practical aspects of community life, and the imperfections he would encounter, in himself and in others, along the road. It was only later, after Cosmas's crisis, that I realized my mistake.

Both his faith and his vocation seemed to be a matter of course. Just as he had never had the slightest doubt about the meaning of his call, so he seemed never to have been at all troubled in his religious beliefs. For him faith was more a state in which he happened to be than a grace or a virtue.

During his last visit, at Pentecost, he talked at long last about his family. He described his marvelous childhood in the huge house in Burgundy in the company of his brother, who was thirteen months older. He told me about his mother, her anxious and melancholy gentleness, her weariness: from her he claimed to have inherited his forehead, pointed nose, and heavy chin, not to mention his attraction to the things of God. He spoke of the exuberant energy and eccentricity of his father, who would come back from his rounds of the farms with pâtés, bottles of wine, and stories that the children hardly understood but that made him laugh as he recounted them. Until the sadly unforgettable day when his brother had said: "Mama is not happy. I've seen her crying twice this week."

Then began—he was about twelve at the time—discoveries of heartbreaking banality. Alone in the room they shared the two boys compared notes and tried out theories. Very soon sly hints from their schoolfellows and the knowing sighs of the maid left them in no doubt as to why their father was so frequently absent and why their mother was so upset.

Yet there was an unexpected event that same year. When they came home from Mass on Sunday morning their mother announced that she was expecting a baby that would probably be born in June. Cosmas remembered desperately hoping that the birth of another child would bring his parents together again, and he prayed with all his heart for this intention. But the birth of a little girl solved nothing. Preoccupied, maudlin, more exhausted than ever, his mother divided her time between caring for the baby and devotions that, although sincere, came close to superstition. Meanwhile the father, although he did not officially leave the family home, was away more and more frequently. When he did occasionally appear, his indifference toward the baby made it perfectly clear that this mishap was none of his business, although he admitted responsibility.

In the middle of the holiday period the elder brother told Cosmas that he could stay in the house no longer; he would give up studying for the baccalaureate and put his name down for a course that prepared students for the art school at Cluny. This plan caused a family row. Despite the disorder of his private life, the father's conscience and professional capacity had not been affected; he remained very devoted to his work as a vet, which had been the tradition in his family for so many generations; and he was outraged that his eldest son should not wish to follow in his footsteps. But the boy would not be moved. So Cosmas remained on his own from now on, cut off from the brother who was almost a twin, caught between an absentee father, a neurotic mother, and a baby sister. The following winter he came to La Trappe for the first time and made the retreat during which, he said, he became aware of his vocation.

When he had finished his story I felt very puzzled. Religious vocations that are too obviously founded on human disappointment—unhappy childhood or adolescence for boys, broken love affairs for girls—are hard to interpret. I've already told you that in some cases such situations can be the means used by the Lord to detach those whom he calls from the world, but they can also be at the origin of bogus vocations.

I raised this matter of ambiguity with Cosmas. He replied that he understood the problem, but that in his case the answer was clear: no doubt these adolescent misfortunes had helped to reveal his vocation, but once he heard the call in this very place, he knew that it had preexisted and that it came from a further and higher level.

So he did his military service and spent his leave either at La Trappe or at home, where he felt increasingly ill at ease. Just after leaving the army he made another retreat. I asked Father Emmanuel to look after him this time, so that we could compare our impressions. I had more confidence in Father Emmanuel than in any of the other monks because I believed that he was the most open to the Holy Spirit, simply and naturally. His luminous, light-blue eyes were a window on his limpid soul. At the same time he had read widely and had a good grasp of psychology. His judgment coincided with mine: Cosmas's vocation was so unproblematic that one couldn't really predict what sort of monk he would be, or what difficulties he would have eventually to face; but that was not a reason for refusing him entry to the noviceship or postponing his entry any longer.

As is our custom, Father Abbot had a long conversation with Cosmas. After leaving the abbot, he came straight to my office. He looked rather worried, and when I asked him if there had been any difficulties he replied: "I don't think so. But Father Abbot wants to talk to you. He's waiting for you now."

Dom Philippe began by asking what I thought. I gave him my diagnosis, and added that it was confirmed by Father Emmanuel.

The abbot, as was his wont, remained silent for a moment and then, slowly opening his pale eyes and looking at me with an intensity that expressed the strength of his inner life, said: "I think it is much more serious than that."

And in answer to my implicit question he added: "Of course we are all searching for the absolute. Unless we had a sense of the absolute, we wouldn't be here leading a life that doesn't add up in human terms. But we know that this search is never ending. That's why the young man I've just seen worries me.

He almost seems to think that as soon as the monastery gates close behind him he will in one leap have reached holiness and deep intimacy with the Lord."

I asked Father Abbot whether his judgment, which although a little pessimistic was not exactly surprising, meant that Cosmas should not be accepted as a novice.

The abbot surprised me by saying that such had indeed been his first thought. Then he added: "But on reflection I think that would be going too far. Tell him that we are prepared to accept him. But you will have a lot to teach him. And first of all he will have to learn that it is God alone, in his infinite patience, who can make us worthy of himself."

I told Cosmas that the abbot had accepted him. Without giving him the comments of Father Abbot in all their harshness, I explained that he must expect to find more difficulties than he had imagined, and that there was a huge gulf between the ideal that brought us to La Trappe in the first place and what our limited strength enabled us to achieve. Once more Cosmas listened to what I had to say respectfully and attentively; but it didn't seem to impinge on him. He went home to put his affairs in order. As he left the abbey, he was filled with an exultant joy. Yet saying good-bye to his parents, brother, and friends took over six weeks: the time he took to move on to the next stage, once his mind was made up, was one of his most surprising and permanent characteristics. He told me that the last conversation he had with his mother was a gloomy business and faintly unreal. His father, who now accepted that neither of his sons would be a vet, concluded his farewell with a phrase that expressed either genuine nostalgia or appalling banality: "You have chosen the better part." His brother was cold and distant, and seemed utterly determined to break with the past. When Cosmas returned to La Trappe at the beginning of November, he insisted once more that henceforward his only family would be the Benedictine family.

Two other postulants entered the abbey at the same time: Jacques Marie, a former naval officer, who was twenty-five years older than Cosmas, and a boy—hardly more than sixteen at the time—who is now Father Louis, the present novice master. He had grown up in a strongly united family, was the only boy after six girls, and he came to La Trappe directly from the minor seminary.

I was now entrusted with the absorbing and yet awe-inspiring task of guiding these three so very different men toward the day when their solemn vows would set the final seal on their response to the Lord's call. I felt a burden of responsibility every time a new group of would-be monks arrived. I prayed that God would make me a faithful guardian of the fruits of his vineyard until harvest time came. But the peaceful assurance that, in that particular year, filled the three postulants, entitled me to hope that the harvest would be abundant.

6

A lifelong commitment to the exclusive service of God is an awesome thing, and it presupposes complete liberty and full knowledge of what one is doing. The transition from secular to monastic life can be shattering even for the most balanced novices who are utterly sure of their vocation: they take time to get adjusted to it and need a period of training. The regularity of our life is a great help, but some of its features—the short time allowed for sleep and the practice of waking up in the middle of the night—are difficult to get used to, and nature continues to rebel. Silence, a simple diet, long periods in choir, mastery over the senses, and an obedience that is not just sporadic but permanent: these are difficult disciplines; and the mind, the will, the whole bodily and nervous system, have to adapt to them. One can never entirely exclude the risk that the shock may be too violent for sensitive souls, inclined to excessive zeal or straining toward heroic virtue, so that when their vocation survives, their health may be impaired.

That is why our Rule and constitutions wisely insist upon a long period of testing before the monk commits himself definitively. This trial period has a number of stages. First come a couple of weeks in the guesthouse, then a month with the community, but in lay dress and as a postulant. The clothing ceremony and the granting of a religious name mark the start of the novitiate proper. Two years and a day later, at the earliest, the monk takes his temporary vows. He has to wait another three years and sometimes longer before committing himself forever with his solemn vows.

Furthermore, it is not the novice himself who decides when he is ready to move on to the next stage. The abbot and his council, and when it comes to solemn vows, the whole community, have to certify that the novice is capable of being a monk for the rest of his life.

The same prudent concern for a gradual adaptation to religious life leads us to pay particular attention to the training of the novices. They are the cherished children of the abbey, within which, gathered round the novice master, they form a privileged community of their own. In the most ancient texts you will find a recommendation to subject the novices to special mortifications and humiliations—just as raw recruits or student freshmen have to go through initiation ceremonies. But that, thank God, no longer happens.

Since there had not been any novices at La Trappe the previous year, I could concentrate entirely on Cosmas and his two companions. I marveled, yet again, at the way the Lord guided three such different characters by his grace, shrewdly and subtly, respecting their differences while leading them to the fulfillment of the same ideal.

Brother Jacques Marie, with his crew cut, prominent nose, tight lips, slightly rolling walk, and firmly belted jacket, was still the naval officer used to action and giving orders. Sometimes he found the Divine Office interminable. Quite obviously the low bows prescribed by the liturgy did not come easily to one who had been trained to stand upright in the wind in his officer's uniform; he bowed rigidly, as though forcing himself. He had a similar intellectual and spiritual stiffness and a certain matter-of-factness. But he passed, easily and naturally, from obedience to orders to obedience to the Rule, and as the weeks went by I was able to observe the almost perceptible workings of grace watering and softening his soul and making it fruitful.

Brother Louis, on the other hand, was hardly out of the awkward stage of adolescence. He was small, could hardly control his limbs, and yet he was just the sort of novice I wanted. God sometimes finds it necessary to impose spiritual trials on people who, like Brother Louis, have been privileged and preserved from childhood onward, and they emerge toughened up and strengthened. But at the time, his only problem was his extreme youthfulness: he found it difficult to concentrate for very long and he could be scatterbrained. I couldn't help smiling in the chapel when he kneeled down instead of bowing, sat down or stood up at the wrong time or after everyone else. But the purity of his heart and the tenderness of his love for Christ and Our Lady bathed him in a glow of light that was almost physically as well as spiritually perceptible.

But I had never seen a novice adapt so quickly and joyously to religious life as Cosmas. The break with his previous life and its involvements seemed to be achieved painlessly and without serious problems.

I can see him now, just before being admitted to the community, placing on Father Secretary's desk the few personal belongings he had brought along. They were to be looked after by Father Secretary, and to give them up was the first step in his renunciation of the world. He had a childhood missal; a coral rosary and a silver statue of Our Lady—gifts he had received on the occasion of his solemn communion; a leather-bound photograph album containing pictures of his parents, his brother, his sister, and a few friends; a wallet; and a badly worn pocketknife. He hesitated over the album, opened it for a moment at the photographs of his mother and much younger sister, and then closed it, emptied his pockets, and smiled at me. It seemed as though he said farewell to his past without any pangs. More than that: he seemed to be glad to be rid of all links with a period that he now wanted to forget.

Father Emmanuel, whom on my advice he had chosen as his confessor and to whom he made a general confession on the eve of the clothing, confirmed this impression. Cosmas's confession of sins committed since childhood obviously brought him great joy: he was joyfully ridding himself of the past as much as he was asking God's forgiveness.

Right from the start he had shown that he had all the proper monastic attitudes. This could be seen in the way he prayed, his instinctive sense for liturgical movements, and in his behavior in the refectory and in chapter. Whether we are tall or short, fat or thin, young or old, the practice of religious life means that sooner or later we come to have an attitude, a way of walking even, that makes the long procession of monks an expression of the community in action. One might have been tempted to say that Cosmas had been practicing for a long time; and sometimes, as I watched him, I thought of a highly gifted actor who was playing the part of a Trappist, and improving on the real thing. But Cosmas, whatever he was, was no actor.

The length of the Divine Office never seemed a burden to him. He was not passionately drawn to study and reading: quite clearly Cosmas was no intellectual but had rather an imaginative and emotional nature. Even so he plodded away at the work he had to do with such application that, given his lack of attraction for study, he was well suited to our way of life: the Trappists are by vocation practical men, and not much concerned with the theoretical knowledge of God; and the time devoted to study is much less than one finds among other Benedictines.

Cosmas was also exemplary in his dealings with his two companions. Whether in the refectory, the study place, or at work on the farm, Cosmas excelled in those little acts of kindness for which community life offers so many opportunities: Brother Louis was too absentminded to notice the need, while Brother Jacques Marie was held back by his rigidity and, perhaps, by the habit of command. Yet both of them admitted to me, each in his own characteristic way, that Cosmas's perfection was an embarrassment but that they were glad of his goodness, his constant smile, and that they loved him like a brother.

I can still see my three novices on the day of their clothing.

The community waited for them in the chapter room. At that time the ceremony had a solemnity that has subsequently been modified. The abbot sat on his throne, raised a few steps above the rest of us, beneath the huge crucifix. He was flanked by the prior and the subprior. Along the walls adorned with the arms of the most famous abbots of La Trappe and the three abbeys founded from Soligny—Thymadeuc; Bellefontaine;

and Tre Fontane, near Rome—stood two rows of monks, the choir monks in their white cowls and the lay brothers in their rough brown habits.

While the novices waited outside, according to custom, I had requested that they should have the right to be admitted to the chapter room. I then led them in, and they were questioned by Father Abbot about their determination to keep our Rule. They confidently gave the ritual answer: "Yes, Father, by the grace of God and with the help of your prayers."

Then they set aside their lay clothes and received the novice's habit that would mark them off from the professed religious for the next two years: a cloak rather than our broad-sleeved habit, a white scapular rather than our black one, a belt of white cloth instead of the leather belt we wore. And finally they received the names they had chosen in religion.

I continued to observe these three men who were and would remain my children throughout the ceremony. I was deeply moved to see how, despite the uniform that made them members of the community, each one retained the personality that he had resolved to consecrate to God and that would enable him to serve God in his own way. Brother Jacques Marie looked even more like a pirate or a bird of prey, and his tense features were strained by his will and emotions. The doll-like face of Brother Louis, who was not yet seventeen, was like that of an altar boy who is a little alarmed at donning a surplice for the first time. Cosmas was radiant with unalloyed happiness, as though he were lost in ecstasy or caught up in a dream.

I remembered how surprised I had been at the council meeting a week earlier when Father Abbot had decided to admit the postulants to the clothing. I had briefly described the characters of each of them and concluded that they should all be admitted. Dom Philippe agreed without comment on Brother Jacques Marie and Brother Louis. But though I had stressed Cosmas's remarkable adaptation to religious life, he said: "I'm afraid he hasn't learned much in six weeks."

7

A clear sky can become clouded over within a few minutes. But at other times one sees only a slight and insignificant white cloud, and then another and another until the whole mass of cloud, suddenly and to one's surprise, blots out the sun.

In a similar way happiness shone in the face of Cosmas from the moment he joined the community; it never left him in the first weeks of his novitiate, and was particularly intense on the day of his clothing; but then, slowly and at first imperceptibly, it departed. A fleeting sadness seemed to come over him for a few seconds, but it vanished so swiftly that one hardly bothered about it: it could be the result of fatigue, worry, or a nostalgic memory of childhood or adolescence.

I thought that physical tiredness was the most likely explanation, all the more when I noticed that the sadness seemed to afflict him just before he set off to work on the farm.

By that time we had already stopped making the chocolate that for many years had kept the community at subsistence level but that latterly had proved catastrophic. We had not yet begun to make cheese, a sort of Port du Salut cheese, which is today our principal source of income along with preserved fruit, eggs, and fresh cream. We were simple farmers. Our main activity was cattle breeding—we sold the beasts ourselves— and milk production. The churns were collected at dawn on behalf of a cooperative in L'Aigle to which we belonged. Our cultivated land was designed to serve the needs of the abbey for flour, vegetables, and fruit and also—most important— to provide food for the cattle. Over and above that we had, as the Rule of St. Benedict suggests, various workshops that enabled us to be self-sufficient. Then as now we had black- smiths, mechanics, and carpenters to look after the upkeep and repair of our agricultural machinery, the buildings, and the furniture. One must also mention Father Marie Bernard's workshop, which mass-produced his statues by some compli- cated method. His statues have been variously judged; they belong to the St.-Sulpice tradition of plaster casts and are too insipid for my taste. But though his artistic skill was question- able, his purity of heart and devotion were boundless: we owe to him the statue of Our Lady of Confidence that watches over the abbey from the hill where we walked the other day and from which one can see how La Trappe is entirely surrounded by forests.

The desire to avoid all distractions meant that even on the farm the novices worked together, usually under the direction of the novice master. But occasionally, as the work on the farm demanded, the novices would be assigned to another working party for a few hours or at most for a few days.

As the son, grandson, and great-grandson of veterinary surgeons, Cosmas was used to animals. He did not need any special instructions in these matters. And yet Cosmas, who adapted to every other duty of monastic life with such rapidity and perfection, seemed to find farmwork more distasteful than the ex-naval officer and his young companion, who was fresh from the minor seminary. Both of them showed a zest for farming that was equaled only by their incompetence. One day Cosmas explained in a rather confused way what it was that troubled him: in another setting and atmosphere he was familiar enough with cows in heat, mating, calving, and other aspects of animal life; but they didn't seem to fit in with his picture of religious life and, in short, seemed shocking in a place of prayer. I used to joke about this, thinking that it was a superficial reaction and not to be taken too seriously. Another time he admitted that this constant reminder of his father's profession worried him, and that in his subconscious the sexual excesses of his father were linked with the mating of the animals.

But he didn't say—and perhaps didn't yet know with any clarity—what most shocked him: the business activity that was the natural consequence of our farming work. A few weeks after he had entered the novitiate, I put him down for half a day with two brothers who were taking a dozen bullocks to the abattoir. Brother Sébastien was the driver. An angry giant of a man, with Herculean strength and a flame red beard, his gestures led one to imagine that, if crossed, he would be capable of bellowing away without breaking silence; but he cared for the engines and drove the lorries with all the sensitive patience of a nurse. He has since been afflicted with sclerosis and the doctor has forbidden him to touch a driving wheel. But he remains in charge of the tractor shed . . . Cosmas sat between him and Brother Maurice, who was in charge of all the abbey's commercial transactions. He died over a year ago. He was our most colorful personality. Rather fat but still lithe and animated, he seemed to be made of India rubber. We used sign language as the ordinary means of communication in the sacristy, the refectory, and at work: he turned it into a virtuoso performance, a puppet show reminiscent of a quarrel between two Neapolitans. He had enriched our sign language with mimes of his own. His hands flew around with astonishing speed. And the most remarkable thing was that even uninitiated strangers understood him: all the cattle dealers and butchers of the area were used to Brother Maurice's sign language. My own deplorable example shows that no monk can resist the temptation to gossip when he gets half a chance: Brother Maurice gossiped in silence. The only exception was the gruff noise he made to confirm the prices that his hands had indicated with the speed and accuracy of a Chinese accountant on his abacus. He was known for miles around as a powerful businessman, and one wondered what job he had before entering the abbey. His girth and his high blood pressure led me to imagine him at table in some provincial hotel, recounting his latest gastronomical discoveries to his fellow commercial travelers. They would have been surprised to learn that, like Father Louis, he had entered La Trappe at sixteen, fresh from a minor seminary, that he detested money, and was one of the most austere of our monks. They would also have discovered that the motive behind his skillful dedication to business was an almost tragic sense of responsibility for the interests of the abbey.

Cosmas knew nothing of that. With baffled astonishment he was the witness of an extraordinarily bitter though silent conversation between Brother Maurice and a cattle dealer. And he was thoroughly scandalized on the way back when Brother Maurice, totally insensitive to the beauty of hills, forests, and lakes in the late autumn sunshine, explained in his mime language that he had got two hundred francs above the current market price. Cosmas was thinking of what the Rule prescribed: "Let the goods always be sold somewhat more cheaply than is done by men of the world, that in all things God may be glorified."

Cosmas, as I could see, felt particularly low that evening. But when I asked him what was the matter he simply said that he was probably mistaken and would rather wait a few days before telling me about it. Perhaps I should have pressed a little harder and gotten him to confide in me there and then. He was so much the perfect novice that I failed to realize how serious and far-reaching the trouble was. But I didn't suspect anything, and neither perhaps did Cosmas himself until the day he told me the story and revealed the deep rift that had opened up between his thoughts and his feelings. Our ordinary life seemed to him to fall increasingly into two distinct parts: there were the hours of prayer in the church, which still brought him happiness; but all the rest of our life distressed him and incurred his disapproval.

Though he only hinted at it, I realized that he simply could not stand work on the farm: it was too earthy and too commercial. And he couldn't bear—this was something I didn't know—meals in the refectory.

The refectory is a place of recollection. You have seen the long hall with its lofty windows and its double row of pointed arches that emerge from the walls and come together on the row of slender pillars down the center. We go there in silence and take up our places at the heavy wooden tables. We sit along the wall, so there is no one opposite to provide a distraction. There is no whispering, and the only sound is the deliberately restrained voice of the reader.

The refectory is also a place of brotherly service. Week by week all the members of the community take it in turns to serve the others. And the Rule prescribes that when we get to our places, we should first see to it that our neighbors have all they need.

The right amount of food is chosen and prepared to remind us that the body is an instrument to be respected and kept in good order; but we are not to be overwhelmed by its demands. It is quite wrong to say that we eat badly at La Trappe. A monk learns to eat slightly less than his appetite demands, but there is no need for him to go hungry, and the style of cooking is plain: without being unpleasant, it does not encourage overeating.

But the refectory is, like the dormitory, a place where the rights of nature cannot be ignored. Our work is strenuous, and this is especially true of those we used to call lay brothers—they now belong to the same category as the choir monks, but they still spend more time than the rest of us in the workshops or on the farm. Throughout the Lenten period, which for us extends almost without a break from the Feast of the Exaltation of the Cross on September 14 to the paschal vigil on Easter Eve, we have only one proper meal a day, apart from a piece of bread in the morning and a snack in the evening. This one meal is obviously rather abundant; and since we don't spend much time over it, the way some of the brethren bolt down their plateful of noodles, rice, potatoes, or beans is not always very refined. Sucking and swallowing noises can sometimes be heard against the monotonous background of the reading.

An experienced monk is not bothered by such details. They seem trivial in the atmosphere of peace, brotherhood, and self-control that reigns in the refectory. But Cosmas had gradually become incapable of judging the relative importance of things. He could no longer see the wood for the trees: the noisy eating habits of a few monks meant that he missed the spiritual significance of our meals.

In the dormitory, too, in the sounding box of his cell, the noises that broke the silence of the night were much more than a mere physical disturbance of his sleep. He saw them as the body's revenge on the soul, the triumph of flesh over spirit.

I observed him carefully: in the mornings he had the drawn features of someone who has not been able to sleep. That was the first really alarming symptom: a monk who can't sleep usually has other problems as well.

Father Alexis's proclamation of faults was yet another factor in Cosmas's breakdown.

This custom, by which a monk denounced the faults of another, has now been suppressed. It used to come after the confession of one's own faults, which took place two or three times a week in the chapter. Perhaps in its thirst for the absolute your generation or the next will revive a tradition that offended our sensibilities only because we had forgotten what it really meant. I've already told you that I dislike military metaphors (I come from a northern working-class family that is traditionally anti-army, while being quite prepared to get killed in war if need be), but that the abbot's council is rather like a general staff. The chapter was the place where the exercise was evaluated once the maneuvers were over. There was no question of commenting on personal failings, which belonged to the sphere of private confession: the accusation was concerned with breaches of the Rule that could become obstacles to the progress of the community as a whole—just as the weakness of a single unit can jeopardize the advance of the entire army. Thus the proclamation of the faults of others was derived from the duty, recognized by French law in other areas, to come to the aid of someone who is in danger: when a monk seemed unaware of his faults or lacked the courage needed to confess them, fraternal charity performed this service on his behalf. It was a way of safeguarding the integrity of community life. But one also had to reckon with the effect on the monk who was accused. Personally I was not sorry to see the custom dropped: its effects could be very good or very bad, depending on the intentions of the "accuser" and the spiritual and mental state of the "accused."

Father Alexis knew nothing of such subtleties. By then he was immensely old, like Rip van Winkle, but his outlook was so outdated that he seemed even older. His intentions were good enough, but he lacked common sense and tended to be excessive in his judgments. He belonged to the old school for whom rebuffs and humiliations were the surest path to holiness. He believed that he was personally responsible for the novices, and was always on the lookout for the slightest failings, which he would then report to the chapter. Twice, within a few days, his broken clarinet of a voice could be heard announcing: "Brother Cosmas fell asleep once again during the Divine Office."

Poor Cosmas could have done without that. I had a word with Father Abbot who asked Father Alexis not to do it again. But the harm was already done, and a crisis now seemed to be unavoidable. Yet I didn't intervene: it is better that novices should get into the habit of confiding spontaneously rather than having to be cross-questioned. But since Cosmas still said nothing, I invited him into my office a few days later, just after chapter, and said: "My son, you're sleeping badly, you look tired, and you've lost that look of habitual joy that cheered us all up so much. And now, though you are usually very trusting, you've been silent for over a week about your problems. What's gone wrong?"

He fell to his knees and said: "Help me, Father—everything's gone wrong."

Though his voice was steady and his Burgundy accent as strong as ever, he seemed utterly exhausted.

"Get up, my son," I said, "and tell me about it."

He poured out his troubles conscientiously, almost painstakingly; though he was in no way frantic, there was a sort of growing apprehension as he discovered that the more he said, the more there remained to say. He described the gulf between the monastic life as he had previously imagined it and its day-to-day reality; he spoke of the contrast between the time spent in prayer in the church and the other activities, which all seemed so remote from any religious ideal.

There was no strain, only a frightening clarity and a hint of excess as he unpacked all his troubles before me. The chewing and swallowing noises in the refectory. Brother Maurice as a dreadful old horse trader. The cattle business, which seemed to him to be just as bad as the buying and selling in the temple at Jerusalem. And in the darkness of the dormitory this diffused, amorphous, all-too-human noise which stopped him finding peace even in sleep.

"So, what next?" I asked.

He fell to his knees again, bowed low, and said: "I didn't think that, apart from the Divine Office, God would be so absent."

I very nearly lost my temper with him. I was so disappointed to see how this young man, whose vocation seemed so well thought out, who had tested it by waiting for several years, and who knew the Rule of St. Benedict almost by heart, should have such a false picture of Cistercian spirituality and such naïveté when confronted with the most elementary difficulties of community life.

I paused for a few moments of silent prayer so as to be able to control my impatience, and then kneeled down alongside Cosmas and said a decade of the rosary with him. Then I asked him to sit down again, and tried to put some sense and order into his thinking.

"I think you are mixing up," I said, "three difficulties of a totally different kind and of unequal importance.

"Nervous exhaustion due to lack of sleep"—and in saying this I realized the mistake we had made in putting him in Denys's Ear, the noisiest cubicle in the dormitory—"can easily be dealt with. If you like you may have leave to sleep in the infirmary for a few days until you can manage to sleep again.

"You also have an obvious distaste for the more down-to-earth side of community life. I don't think that is very serious. When you were doing your military service you must have seen and heard far worse than that . . ."

He interrupted me to say: "Of course, Father, but that wasn't at La Trappe."

This time, I must admit, his stupidity made me lose my temper. I reminded him, rather brusquely, that Trappists were recruited from among men and not angels. If he were incapable of putting up with the physical presence of the brethren, then perhaps he would be better off as a Carthusian, a hermit, or an anchorite like St. Simeon on his pillar. And if the behavior of some of the lay brothers offended his delicate feelings, he would probably be better off as a vet looking after cats and poodles in a fashionable suburb.

This mention of his family and indirectly of his father, together with the suggestion that he might possibly return to lay life, were too much for Cosmas's nerves. His shoulders heaved. He leaned forward, buried his head in his hands, and shook with sobbing.

I blamed myself and asked God's forgiveness while waiting for the moment of crisis to pass. It seemed to me to be not a bad thing that it should happen like this.

When at last Cosmas had calmed down and began to look at me again, I apologized for my ill temper and did my best to reassure him. There was nothing unusual about such difficulties. Many novices before him had been tried in the same way. It was a matter of getting used to things.

"You're tough enough," I said with a smile, "and healthy enough to win through . . . The only serious thing is that you don't seem to understand the profound and balanced unity of religious life as St. Benedict conceived it. Can't you see that to think that the service of God is limited to the Divine Office and that, for all the rest of the time, man takes over, is a gross misunderstanding of religious life?

"Driving the animals to the fields or to the abattoir, plowing a field, eating, sleeping—these are all forms of prayer that are just as good as liturgical prayers, the Gloria, or the psalms, provided that all these tasks, even the humblest and most material, are carried out in a spirit of obedience to the Rule and to superiors and, through them, to the will of God. These truths are obvious to anyone who reads the Rule of St. Benedict. Have you forgotten it now, my son, you who knew the Rule by heart even before you crossed the threshold of La Trappe? Or have you subconsciously adapted it to suit yourself, to make it the rule of another life, which is not ours?"

I gathered my thoughts again for a few moments, afraid that I might give way to irritation once more: why did I have to teach such basic lessons to a novice of Cosmas's caliber?

When I was sure that I had regained my composure, I gently reminded him that St. Benedict wanted a balanced, natural, and humane life for his sons, even if living it to perfection involved ever-renewed effort and self-forgetfulness. I reminded him how suspicious the church had always been of those with utopian or illuminist illusions. I emphasized that the only officially recognized mystics were men and women who had both feet firmly on the ground. I had the works of St. John of the Cross to hand—I was rereading him just then as part of some study project. To a Carmelite nun who had to deal with the Jesuits over the sale of a house, he had written with great frankness: "Do not trust the good fathers when their interests are at stake. If they mention a price that suits you, get the contract signed immediately." Wasn't that on a par with Brother Maurice's haggling with the cattle merchants?

I'd hoped that this might raise a smile. But Cosmas tried to explain: "What really shocks me," he said, "is not the farmwork itself, nor the fact that the monks remain subject to human needs and servitudes. The point is that in all these areas I expected to find a greater difference between those who remain in the world and those who spend long hours in prayer and whose lives are dedicated to God's service."

I confined myself to pointing out that this impression was radically mistaken and advised him not to pay any attention to it until he was calmer and able to sleep properly. I ordered him to sleep in the infirmary that very evening.

The bell was summoning us to the church for Vespers. When they were over, I asked to speak to Father Abbot. He listened to me in his usual way, erect as ever, all the upper part of his body—the shoulders, the stiff neck, and the impassive face—remaining astonishingly still; I gave him a detailed account of my conversation with Cosmas, not forgetting the impatience to which I had given way and for which I asked forgiveness. A tight-lipped smile came over Father Abbot and he murmured, without looking up from beneath his heavy eyelids, "I understand you, Father . . ."

I finished my story, and Father Abbot said nothing for a moment. Then he slowly opened his eyes and gave me a look that was somehow both noncommittal and shrewd. But he cast his eyes down again before asking: "What do you propose to do now? I always felt that this would be a difficult case."

Anyone who knew Dom Philippe well would have realized that this interrogative answer and mention of difficulties revealed a hesitancy far removed from his usual style. On the other occasions—they were rare—when he had seemed to be at a loss, I had felt a flood of affection for him: he seemed so terribly self-possessed, and yet he could also be very vulnerable. Despite the solid façade he presented, one felt there could be a breach through which a little light and warmth might just make their way. I would have liked my voice to convey something of the filial affection I felt . . . But he continued to listen impassively with his eyes still closed.

"In my opinion," I said, "the first thing is to make sure he gets some sleep. That's why I've already told him to sleep in the infirmary for a few days. We'll soon see whether we are dealing with nervous exhaustion or a deeper crisis. When we know the facts we can decide what to do."

Father Abbot remained deep in silent recollection for what seemed a long time. That was also typical of this attractive but disconcerting man: the lips did not stir, the whole face remained motionless, but one knew that he was praying. He looked up at me again and said, gravely: "I'm afraid that won't be enough. He may seem to have found inner peace once again, but it won't be a real cure. We have to take advantage of this crisis to remove the cause of the trouble."

I thought that Dom Philippe meant that Cosmas should be sent away from the abbey for good, and began to plead his cause. But Father Abbot interrupted me:

"That would perhaps be the wisest course, but I'm not convinced enough that my diagnosis is correct to take so radical a decision. What we have to do, Father, is insist that Cosmas should undergo another trial period, away from the abbey, and in this way he will be able to sort out his ideas on religious life and—more important still—learn to assess his own feelings. He certainly *wants* to share our life: I'm not sure that he understands what it really means or whether he has the strength of will to persevere without wearying and to remain fully open to the grace of God."

I asked whether he would like to see Cosmas or his spiritual director, Father Emmanuel, before confirming the decision that Cosmas should be dismissed. He said that would no longer be necessary, now that he had made up his mind. He added: "It's a decision that brings me great sadness."

I was just about to leave when suddenly it came to me how distressed Cosmas would be at having to give up his novice's habit. I began to intercede for him, but the abbot stopped me before I could get under way. He turned toward me and without opening his eyes said: "You sought my advice, Father, and now you have it."

Authority intervened between Dom Philippe and myself with the finality of the guillotine.

Cosmas was informed that he would have his evening meal in his room, that he could be present at Compline and Vespers but was dispensed from Matins, and that I would see him early in the morning after terce.

He obeyed these orders. Later that evening I saw him in the obscurity of the church, but there was no indication of his deeper feelings. The next morning I went along to the infirmary where he was resting in bed. Brother Infirmarian said that he had had a disturbed night, but even so I was surprised to see how calm he was. If he hadn't himself spoken of his collapse the previous evening and the distress it had caused him, I might have thought I'd been the victim of a nightmare or a hallucination.

I was rather disconcerted by the way he took Father Abbot's decision that he should leave La Trappe for a few months; it flashed through my mind that he was rather relieved at the idea. I went back to the infirmary in the afternoon. By now he was up and dressed in his novice's habit. We ran through in complete tranquility the plan for this trial period and the experiments he would undergo. When everything was sorted out, he asked me to spend a few minutes with him in the church before the Blessed Sacrament; and then, as we left the church, he kneeled down and asked for a special blessing. As he arose, he said simply and with great feeling: "Thank you, Father. I have a feeling that these months will be long and hard. But I can see the light at the end of the tunnel."

He took a few steps away from me and then turned back to face me: "Father, couldn't I . . . ?"

His eyes ran down his novice's habit.

I shook my head and said no. We couldn't allow anyone to keep his religious habit. Cosmas looked sad and inconsolable; but he smiled as though to say that he accepted that as well.

Did this total and almost joyful obedience prove that he was a true Cistercian? Had Father Abbot misjudged him? Or on the contrary . . . ? The word *relief* flashed into my mind once more.

8

Cosmas left La Trappe by the first bus at dawn the next day. At Mass the abbot included his name among the special intentions in the Memento of the Living: "We pray that the spirit of God may enlighten the mind of our brother Cosmas."

The two remaining novices, the sailor and Brother Louis, asked no questions, and I was glad that their apprenticeship in religious discretion was so far advanced. But I'm quite sure that they—and the other brothers—understood perfectly well the reasons for this temporary departure. Men of silence come to know things by intuition more swiftly and deeply than talkative people.

As I came out of the church I met Brother Marie Gabriel, who was in charge of the wardrobe. He had returned Cosmas's civilian clothes and taken away his novice's habit. To my knowledge Brother Marie Gabriel was the only monk who had almost never—perhaps actually never—asked for leave to speak. He managed to extend the range of our sign language by marvelously expressive mime. He even outclassed Brother Maurice, our cattle dealer. A dry little cough served for punctuation. He made an open-handed gesture, and followed it up with lip movements that meant that he had something to tell me. He pointed toward the infirmary, stretched out his hands, and then folded them on his chest to indicate the cape worn by the novices, adopted the desolate air of a man on the verge of tears, but corrected this impression by passing his hand across his face and gently smiling. It wasn't difficult to guess that he was describing Cosmas's sadness when he had to exchange his scapular and cape for the jacket he was wearing on his arrival, and how he finally accepted the situation. I nodded to show that I understood. Brother Marie Gabriel looked very pleased and, quiet as a mouse, trotted off.

But I was still thinking about Cosmas. By now he would be in Paris, going from the Gare Montparnasse to the Gare de Lyon.

I told you that we spent the previous day arranging his program. He said that he did not want to go back to his family, and I thought that was wise. We agreed that he would ask to stay with one of his former teachers, now living in retirement in a Morvan village. There he could rest for as long as necessary and be examined by a doctor from Clamecy whom he trusted. The doctor would ascertain whether his nervous system and general balance had been affected. After which he would try to join a group ministry team in a parish so as to know and understand the life of a diocesan priest.

I also advised him to try to learn more, by short visits if need be, about other religious orders and especially about the other branches of the Benedictine family, for whom the farmwork he found so shocking was less important. He very properly replied that he was not in the least an intellectual and that it wasn't the time devoted to material work that worried him so much as the spirit in which it was done. On the other hand, he took up eagerly my half-joking suggestion that he should spend some time with the Carthusians. So I gave him two letters of recommendation, one for the bishop of Autun and the other for the prior of the Selignac charter house, who happened to be friends of mine. Finally I had suggested that he should have some experience of lay life, perhaps by doing some professional work for a short time. Cosmas refused. He conceded that it was just possible that a setting other than La Trappe and a rule other than the Cistercian rule might enable him to fulfill his vocation, but he would not hear of any questioning of the only certainty that had never left him even in his darkest moments: that he was destined for the exclusive service of God.

We also agreed that Cosmas would write occasionally to let me know how he was faring and to ask for advice should he feel the need to. With unfailing regularity he wrote a letter—a very long letter—at the end of each month. I've kept the entire correspondence, and you can see for yourself how bulky it is.

If I read you a few paragraphs I'm sure you will sense the unconscious and instinctive ambivalence of Cosmas's behavior. Of course, he had made up his mind to give himself a fair test and loyally to accept the consequences of the experiment to which he had consented. But in what spirit? In the depths of his heart, what did he really expect from this trial period? Light on the sort of life he was called to? Or supporting arguments in favor of a preestablished truth? Was he trying to discover whether he had a vocation to La Trappe? Or did he merely wish to convince us that he was destined for this life?

I'm astonished now, with hindsight, that I was not more anguished by these questions when I first read the letters. Why was it that I was neither surprised nor alarmed by the fact that Cosmas's letters never really expected an answer and never asked for advice? They were positive and descriptive, and they never asked questions. I could have confined myself to noting their arrival and thanking him. The stray thoughts and suggestions in my replies always came on my own initiative: they had never been invited.

Here for example is the beginning of one of Cosmas's letters written a few months after his departure when he was working in a small town, not far from Autun, as lay helper to a parish priest who was without a curate:

My dear Father,

I am now settled in my work as substitute curate here in Morvan. There's nothing much to be said about my state of health. I've seen the doctor who has once again examined me thoroughly. I am pronounced sound in body and in mind, and the nervous troubles that made me leave La Trappe have had no aftereffects.

You'll be wanting to know about my recent state of mind . . .

We all have our verbal mannerisms. Cosmas wrote as he spoke and as I read his letters I could almost hear him rolling his *r*'s as Burgundians habitually do.

You'll be wanting to know about my recent state of mind. Everything is going well. I sometimes long for the sky-scapes of Le Perche and feel very impatient. But don't worry, Father. I'm not challenging the timetable that we agreed upon.

I spend my time in much the same way as I described in my last letter: teaching catechism to the children, looking after the fabric of the church, attending meetings of a group of young people—fifteen or so girls and a dozen boys out of a parish of twelve hundred. But I spend more time than before on cooking and housekeeping for the parish priest.

He has no maid, but a rather useless and unkempt char-woman comes in two mornings a week.

On a deeper level I'm increasingly alarmed by the life led by these secular priests. Alarmed and yet filled with compassion. They are so lonely and so powerless. Truisms, I know. But I didn't realize just how accurate they were.

For most of the people in the village the parish priest is no more than a provider of services. The mechanic mends cars; the baker bakes bread; the parish priest baptizes the children and teaches them the catechism up to their solemn communion; he blesses weddings and funerals and sings High Mass every Sunday even though there is practically no one there. That's all he does. You may say that I should have known all this, since I spent my childhood in this part of France. Frankly I didn't realize what it was like. My parents used to invite their parish priest two or three times a year. A few families here do the same. But once they have got this act of courtesy out of the way, they won't have the priest interfering in their lives, least of all their private lives. Would you believe it, Father, but I heard a neighboring parish priest praised because "he left everyone alone"?

In such a situation how can a priest really rouse his parish and preach the gospel? I told you a couple of months ago that my parish priest is an old man with long white hair and cheeks as ruddy as apples. He's still very fit for his age. But he's completely worn out. He has lived alone for so long that he's lost the knack of talking at meals. Even so, the odd phrase comes tumbling out. The other day, during coffee, he suddenly said: "Look here, young man, I've been in this parish for more than twenty years and I haven't been able to change a single thing: all the messiness that was here when I came is still here; what little good there was has not progressed, and God is as unimportant to them as ever he was."

A few months ago I might have thought he was incompetent. Now I know that it is not his fault. Someone like St. Bernard could move mountains of indifference. An ordinary priest, even if he is a good priest, simply can't. You will no doubt think, Father, that I'm painting too gloomy a picture, that priests in city parishes are less isolated and that there are areas where pastoral work still makes sense. Maybe that's true, but it seems to me that a priest must always have this same feeling of powerlessness.

I thank the Lord daily that he called me to religious life where one doesn't have to exhaust one's strength in action, and where one can rely on God through prayer and contemplation.

Please don't think I feel superior to the secular clergy. The few weeks I've spent here have increased my admiration for them. One would have to be a model monk even to begin to deserve comparison with a priest in a country or a working-class parish. And every day at La Trappe I will pray with all my heart and ask Christ to give his priests the tremendous courage that they need.

But I couldn't be a secular priest.

You may conclude that my attraction to the cloistered life is partly a matter of cowardice. It could be, Father, and I accept that with humility. But all I can say is that I would be unable to lead the sort of life led by my parish priest and his colleagues. I have Mary's vocation, not Martha's.

I'll spare you the end of the letter. Cosmas simply confirmed that he proposed to leave the village as soon as the bishop sent the promised curate. Then, still sticking to our arrangements, he would spend a few weeks with the Carthusians at Selignac.

I passed the letter on to Father Abbot. When he returned it the next day, all he said was: "He'll come back to us—I've known that since the day he left. But I'm less confident about the value of this absence. And anyway, in the end . . ."

I paused in silence, waiting for some further explanation. But the abbot was expecting a visitor and evidently felt that he had said enough.

In my reply to Cosmas I advised him to try to reach a more careful and balanced judgment. It was too naive to contrast religious and secular as Martha and Mary. He would have to learn and foster the deep spirituality and intimacy with Christ that can be found in parish life. And whether God grants the prayers of monks or rewards the labor of the diocesan priest, it is always God and God alone who is really effective.

Yet I was deeply troubled by the abbot's pessimism about Cosmas's future.

Long experience had taught me to recognize the subtlety and psychological penetration of Dom Philippe's judgments. And the crisis we had to deal with justified the caution manifested by the abbot when Cosmas came to La Trappe and when he took the habit. But I thought that he was at least premature and probably overexaggerating in suggesting that Cosmas was incapable of progress. I knew that I was myself partly responsible for his difficulties. If I had noticed the warning signals and got him to share his burden with me at the right moment, before he lost control of his nerves, then things would not have come to a head in such a critical way.

So I felt bound to do everything that was humanly possible, with the help of God's grace, to enable Cosmas to return to the community where he would find the peace and joy that he sought. In any case, the novice master always tends to defend his novices. And finally I have to admit that, despite the filial obedience and the deep admiration I had for the abbot, the difference in our characters, social background, and cast of mind meant that my first reaction was very often to want to contradict him.

With the help of prayer and meditation I tried in the next few weeks to understand more clearly Cosmas's situation, and to discover why he had made such heavy weather of difficulties that, after all, are not uncommon and that every postulant has to face sooner or later: the crumbling of the illusions that were encouraged by an overidealistic or unreal conception of monastic life, and having to accept the humbler aspects of common life. Why had all this become so fraught for Cosmas? What were the grounds for Dom Philippe's apprehensions? And how could I help Cosmas, on his return, to show that these apprehensions were unfounded?

I remembered the other young men whom I still carried in my heart. They had had to leave the noviceship after a few weeks or a few months.

There was the charming and gentle François. His delicate and sensitive nature gave him a taste for silence and personal prayer, and his limpid soul was made for intimacy with Christ and Our Lady. But, alas, he was burdened with a terrible alcoholic heritage, which meant that his nervous system was too fragile for the trials of community life.

Then there was another François, ardent and generous, who had a real talent for music and painting but who hadn't the courage—or more simply the trust in God—to face the painful trial of chastity for the rest of his life.

I thought of Ambroise, so remarkably intelligent, and of the admirable Georges, who was incapable of half measures. Their going made me terribly sad because it meant that grace had been unable to overcome their pride. They both felt wounded in their pride—Ambroise, when he became aware of his own weaknesses and the length of the road ahead; Georges, because he discovered and judged the imperfections of the community. They both thought of a religious vocation as something quite exceptional and—this was especially true of Ambroise—felt that their ability to respond to it prevented them from accepting humble human realities in themselves and in others. I tried in vain to transform this pride into a more modest form of the desire for holiness. Repeatedly disillusioned, they had both fallen into dryness and bitterness.

But none of these considerations seemed to apply to Cosmas's difficulties. He was neither neurotic nor mentally ill nor obsessed with sex: his temptations and his way of dealing with them were thoroughly normal and healthy. He, too, had been disillusioned, but his pride was not injured. I don't mean to say that he had no pride—is anyone completely free of it?— but his simplicity, directness, and the way he had let himself go in my office proved that he was certainly not excessively proud. This was confirmed by the way his letters clearly showed his admiration for the diocesan clergy, even though he knew he was destined for a different vocation. The proud almost always behave like the fox in the fable when he sees the grapes he cannot reach: they disparage what they cannot have.

Maybe it could all be much more simply explained by Cosmas's lack of maturity and by the results of his upbringing. There was still something rather childish about him; and that could make it rather difficult for him to discard the rose-tinted spectacles through which he looked out on life. As he read and reread the Rule of St. Benedict, he had probably more or less drawn it into his own private vision of monastic life, emphasizing some features while underplaying others, disturbing the balance of the whole, and thus, in the end, preparing the disillusionment that had broken him.

He had inherited from his mother a special love for devotional practices, and that explained his one-sided desire to spend hours in church. By "special love" I mean a natural and human inclination for this kind of thing, which is a very different matter from a truly religious disposition. And his father's disorderly life could be expected to lead him to look for some kind of compensation. When young people discover one of their relations involved in scandalous behavior, they react either by emulating or opposing them. As the son of an inadequate husband, Cosmas naturally felt called to a high level of religious life. That would also explain his distaste for the mediocre aspects of monastic life.

I felt relieved when I had summed things up in this way. Cosmas's crisis was conventional enough and unusual only in its violence. It had no special cause but was understandable in terms of what scientists call *resonance:* the sudden and violent amplification of sounds weak in themselves that results from chance and coincidence. That did not seem to me to be serious enough to prevent Cosmas, on his return, from becoming the excellent monk that he had looked like being at the start of his religious life.

In his letters Cosmas continued to argue strongly for the genuineness of his Cistercian vocation. Here, for example, is an extract from the last letter he wrote, shortly before he left the parish near Autun:

. . . Something happened yesterday. An old seminary friend of my parish priest came to lunch. He's a Holy Ghost Father who has a parish of several hundred square miles somewhere in the middle of Africa.

This time I really had my fill! If providence wanted to show me that my place is at La Trappe and not elsewhere, no one could have put me off the active life more than this splendid Holy Ghost Father. All right, I know that we are no longer in the heroic age in which missionaries are tortured. But even so, I expected something different. If only you'd heard him. Endless trivial stories about precedence and rivalry between headmen. They made the jealousies among our pious women seem derisory.

You know the conclusion that I draw from all this, Father: with all my heart and all my soul I belong, completely and exclusively, to La Trappe.

For the first time since Cosmas's departure I failed to receive a letter at the end of the following month. When a letter did eventually arrive, it contained the first hint that Cosmas had perhaps been touched by a slight doubt:

My dear Father,

You nearly ruined my life. I was completely won over by the Carthusians and was tempted to stay longer. Thanks to your recommendation the prior assigned me an empty cell and let me share fully in the life of the monks. In the first few days I thought that I had been mistaken in going to La Trappe and that my true vocation was to the Carthusians. I found the Carthusian life more balanced and better suited to my tastes than the Cistercian life. What it comes down to is that the community assembles only for the night office, Mass, and Vespers. For the rest of the time each one communes with God and himself. I very nearly found here a rationale for my revolt against some features of common life at La Trappe.

But I must tell you what happened next. I soon realized that this solitary prayer and meditation needed a strength of character and an ability to concentrate that I simply don't have. You've guessed it: I was daydreaming. But let me assure you that my illusions about myself have been shattered: I'm completely unable to live on my own for more than a few weeks; my life needs a well-ordered framework and, above all, I need other people.

As the days slipped by, something extraordinary happened. All the bad memories of La Trappe came back to me in great detail and yet completely transformed. How can I put it, Father? They had a different feel, a different coefficient. You know how overawed and troubled I am by the physical strength of Brother Sébastien. Well, all I could see was the gentleness with which he approached his tractors and cars. The dry cough of Brother Marie Gabriel used to irritate me during office; but in my memory it began to sound almost like the tinkling of a homely little bell. I could see as though I were actually present those hooded forms coming and going about the daily routine I knew so well—the tall and the short, the slim and the stout, like Brother Yves and yourself, Father! I could put a name to each of them and felt drawn just as I had been fourteen years ago when I first went to La Trappe.

I am so grateful to you, Father, for letting me have this experience, even if the idea was partly a joke on your part. I now know that I need community life, despite the depressing aspects of it. They say that boys who are troublesome at home prefer schools with a strict discipline because they feel that it's good for them. That just about sums up my situation: I need a framework for my life, and I need the help of others.

You may well say that I could have discovered all this without ever leaving La Trappe. True, it all seems obvious to me now. But how could I have understood it immediately after I left? And, anyway, it was the abbot himself who told me to leave.

The point is that by the grace of God and with the help of St. Benedict and St. Bernard I am your son forever.

My first impulse was to write and tell him that we were now ready to welcome him back with great joy. But first I went to ask Father Abbot for leave to write to Cosmas and inform him of our acceptance of him. Dom Philippe skimmed through the letter, looked at me for a moment, and said with dry humor: "May I point out, Father, that he hasn't asked for our opinion?" Then he relaxed. Just as on the evening when I had talked to him of Cosmas's crisis, I felt that his customary assurance was somewhat undermined. He added, with a slight hint of hesitation: "It's funny. I've always had a feeling that this boy was not made to live here. But I have to admit that the strength of his conviction is impressive. What's your view, Father?"

I gave Dom Philippe the results of my lengthy reflections on Cosmas and explained the optimistic conclusion I had reached.

He looked at me rather dubiously, a skeptical smile forming on his lips; then he shook his head to indicate that I had not convinced him completely and, as usual, shut his eyes before delivering his verdict: "Perhaps this will surprise you," he said—and his words were indeed surprising, coming from a man of such eminence—"but I don't feel capable of deciding for you. Act according to your conscience; and may God guide you."

After this conversation I felt the need to pray for a long time before writing to Cosmas to say that we were expecting him back at La Trappe.

I thought that he would return, or at least fix the date of his return, as soon as he received my letter. But he replied rather oddly that he wanted to visit a few more abbeys before coming here.

What could this mean? Was he becoming one of those wandering monks, traveling around from monastery to monastery, whom St. Benedict treated rather roughly and called *gyrovagi?* Was it another instance of something I had already noted in his character: the way he paused between taking a decision and carrying it out? Or was he still heaping up yet more arguments to persuade himself that his place was here and could not be elsewhere?

The three or four letters I received in the next few weeks seemed to support this interpretation. They said practically nothing about the spiritual atmosphere of the monasteries in whose guesthouses he spent a few days. He described their setting and surroundings in rather disparaging terms and, by contrast, enthused over the beauty of our landscapes in Le Perche.

They were superficial letters, and yet I read them with sympathy. The love of nature, in which we all have to live, has always seemed to me to be a helpful feeling; and I think that God is always ready to use the beauties of creation to draw men along his paths. In your walks here you have seen for yourself the charm of Le Perche. Each season offers a different facet of beauty. The more one lives here, the more one comes under the spell of its mysterious grace. The forests and woods, once marshland, that the early monks drained and turned into a rosary of lakes. The mists of evening and early morning. The ruddy glow of the tracks and the dramatic gash of the quarries whose sandstone makes up the walls of the houses. The russet tiles that glow in the setting sun. The autumns that catch fire with magical color. The gentle, unpredictable springs. The secretive winters when the cattle steam as they lie down on the yellowing grass, well protected by their rough furry coats, overshadowed by the deep purple of the forests. And the springs that bubble up on all sides and set off, haphazardly, for the valley of the Loire or the Seine or make directly for the Normandy coast. Whatever the administrators and map-makers might say, we are not really in the Île-de-France nor in Normandy nor in Maine. A region is always reluctant to let anyone else have control of its springs and streams, which is why Le Perche managed to remain independent for so long. Forgive, once again, my talkativeness and forgive this lyrical outburst. I come from the north, from near Cambrai. But this patch of earth and sky is now my earthly home.

Cosmas came back one afternoon. His return was as discreet as his departure. A religious community has a great capacity for welcoming those who return. When one of the brothers comes back, no matter how long he has been away and whatever the cause of his absence, everyone behaves as though he had left just a few minutes before. It is as though an object slides down into the water, with hardly a ripple.

Father Abbot agreed with my request that Cosmas should resume his novice's habit without any further delay.

9

Cosmas had made a good start. Circumstances helped him. A community is a living reality: its routine and steady continuity in work, the single goal constantly pursued, the ever-renewed search for the divine presence, do not abolish all light and shade. Sometimes complicated and interrelated problems seem to be resolved quite naturally, and then we feel the grace of monastic life; but at other times we begin to feel how oppressive and irksome it can be.

The monk is taught to mistrust these fluctuating feelings. Yet if it is true that our peace and our joy are not merely a skin-deep happiness but flow from our harmony with the will of God and the concord of the brethren, then why shouldn't we savor such encouraging feelings?

Even St. John of the Cross, who emphasized more than anyone the need to renounce sensible satisfactions, cannot bring himself to deny their spiritual value completely. I was rereading the other day the passage in *The Dark Night* where he speaks of the wonderful to-and-fro movement to which truly detached souls are invited. Led by a desire for mystical purity, he says again and again for page after page that our prayer is weak indeed if our fervor depends upon the beauty of the church or the quality of the music or the talent of the preacher. And then, all of a sudden, after exhorting us to the most complete abnegation, he adds: if the intensity of your prayer no longer depends on architecture or music or eloquence, if you pray just as well in the most ghastly of chapels as in the finest cathedral, just as well whether the choir is made up of braying wretches or of angelic voices, just as well listening to the most banal or the most inspired sermon, then what a grace it is to enjoy to the full, as a bonus, all the splendors of architecture, music, and sacred eloquence.

In his great humanity our holy Father St. Benedict would have appreciated that conclusion. I'm sure he would have accepted, as nourishment for our spiritual joy, the almost tangible sense of happiness and completion that we were living through at that time.

We had the most wonderful sunlit summer, perhaps the finest since I came here. Dominique was back again, with his southern accent, so rare in Le Perche, which seemed to bring the sun with it. We were putting the finishing touches to the frightful silage tower and yet, appalling and pretentious though it was, building it brought a sense of exultation. The title of builders, frequently applied to monks, is especially apt for Benedictines. To build a church or a monastery, a hospital or a guesthouse, a road or a bridge, to dig a ditch or build up the dam of a lake—these are tasks we accomplish in a spirit of gratitude: we feel called by the Lord to perfect his creation.

I hesitate to say it, but the attitude of Father Abbot seemed to be modeled on that of heaven. It is no doubt irreverent to speak of moods in a superior and certainly inappropriate in the case of Dom Philippe, who had reached a rare degree of self-mastery. But the practice of silence gives us a sixth sense, comparable to that of the blind: because we speak so little we sense things out with keener antennae. All the brethren noticed the increasing gentleness of Father Abbot. I've already told you about the great respect, admiration, and filial affection he inspired in us; but he also aroused feelings of awed shyness, not to say fear. And now there were certain discreet hints—in the tone of voice, in the wasted word no longer withheld, and in his unprecedented moderation in punishing faults against the Rule—that led us to believe not exactly that he was changing but that he was becoming slightly less unyielding in his behavior. Was there perhaps some respite from the pain that tortured him? Or, on the contrary, had he been told that his disease was incurable and that he had only a few more years to live among us, and so wanted to let us glimpse his real feelings before taking leave of us?

The brothers were at peace with one another. You might think that feelings are repressed and muffled in our recollected life. Just the opposite is true. Fraternal charity helps us to overcome as best we can the attractions and aversions that we feel for one another. But they remain all the same, and the community is aware of these affinities, misunderstandings, irritations, and sometimes even hostilities and jealousies. The ordered regularity of our life means that a monastery is like a sounding box. Incidents that elsewhere would be submerged in the flow of daily events take on special importance here, just as the slightest sound is amplified in the silence of the night. At the beginning of the year the abbot had made some changes in the assignment of work, and this had caused tensions. A formed religious can easily accept removal from a particular office; but it becomes harder to accept when the work is then given to a brother in whom he has no confidence or toward whom, for whatever reason, he bears a grudge. But the graces received on all sides soon banished these dark clouds: those who had previously held the offices in question admitted that the abbot had made shrewd appointments; and those entrusted with new jobs helped everyone to forget about their promotion and set about proving their worthiness by their competence, punctuality, and humility.

As for me, the post of novice master brought great consolation. I was like a father who watches his sons walk gaily along the path of holiness. During the eighteen months that Cosmas had been away, the other two postulants had made giant strides, and the abbot had fixed for their temporary vows as early a date as the constitutions allow—that is, two years and a day after taking the habit. I've told you that I don't much like military metaphors, which comes from the period when Christian kings were the church's secular arm. And yet such images—knight and soldier of Christ—sprang inevitably into my mind as I observed the way Brother Jacques Marie, a true and sturdy soul, strode along the path of Cistercian perfection. This former sailor had not stopped being an officer when he became a monk. As for his companion, Brother Louis, I knew how much fervor and zeal were needed to adapt so easily to monastic life. But Brother Louis, frail as he was, was one of those souls who are blessed with an unshakable and unspectacular courage.

Was all this peace just an accident? Was it the effect of the wonderful summer we had enjoyed, all aglow with delicate sunlight, with none of the sultry storm-laden heat that so often accompanies fine weather in these parts? Or did the state of grace in which the community was mysteriously living overflow and affect others outside it? During those two months an unprecedented number of visitors made their way to La Trappe. The porter had more than once had to turn back women who tried to enter the enclosure disguised as men. The

benches at the back of the church, which were open to the public, were packed for the High Mass every Sunday morning.

You know about the retreatants we have here, a continual
coming and going of individuals and groups, laymen or priests,
young or old. There are also those "men of goodwill," some of
them unbelievers like yourself, who come to meditate on the
meaning of their life in this peaceful atmosphere. That year
the guesthouse beat all records. We had to improvise. A little
village of tents grew up among the apple and cherry orchards
on the banks of de Rancé Lake.

The building to the right of the main porch—it contains
the parlors and the guests' chapel—was never empty. You
know that this is where the rare female visitors that the Rule or
the superior allow—mothers, sisters, and, exceptionally, more
distant relatives—are received; there, too, visiting priests say
Mass, unless they are specially invited into the abbey church;
and there the few feasts to which a religious may invite members of his family are celebrated in prayer together—the golden
jubilee of a profession, the anniversary of priestly ordination,
or someone's death. This is where some of the monks hear confessions and look after the faithful who live in the area; and
it is where we receive souls in distress who want to rid themselves at a stroke of the burden of anxiety or shame or obses-
sions or scruples. It is a difficult ministry in which the cockle
and the good seed are intermingled. Many of these chance

penitents depart as they came, still drifting with the current. Sometimes we have the great joy of helping a few to make their way upstream and to find a firm foothold. Two of the monks who today live and pray with us arrived just like that, mysteriously guided by providence, dissatisfied with themselves as they were, and so they never left this haven of mercy where they found peace.

Visiting priests, the monks' families, regular or occasional penitents, wives and daughters praying in the chapel while their husbands and fathers visited the abbey—these men and women at every level of faith, from mere tourists to those close to the community, kept up a constant buzz of activity and conversation around the abbey. But our religious life was not disturbed.

We are more used than you might think to shutting out the clamor of the world without being cut off from it. There is a totally false image of the contemplative as an introverted person, so lost in his permanent conversation with God that he ignores the concerns of other people and despises those who rush around outside while he gets on with praying in the peace of the cloister. The love of God and one's neighbor, which no Christian can separate, are linked with especial closeness in the heart of a monk. The religious offers to the Lord his secluded life of prayer, sacrifice, and work for all men and for their salvation. It is not at all paradoxical that

Thérèse of Lisieux, immured in her Carmelite convent, should have become the patron of the missions. To help those who do not really understand our vocation, we like to quote the remark of the young woman who joined the Trappist nuns: she did this, she explained, so that her love could have still greater influence.

The whole community is aware of contemporary events, crises, and ideas—as Father Abbot determines—and learns to respond to them in its own characteristic way, which is that of prayer and penance. It could, of course, happen that news of conflicts outside could prove disruptive in a community that was already suffering from internal tensions or undergoing a period of crisis. But so long as there is balanced harmony in a community outside factors nourish our prayer and meditation without disturbing our peace. We welcome them, we offer them to the Lord, but we try to be like those transparent crystals that allow the colors to pass through them but are not themselves affected. So, throughout this summer, we prayed to God daily for all those who had come to the abbey, whatever their motives: and this extra burden of intentions enriched our prayer without distracting our minds. We felt not so much that we were being dragged into the everyday world but rather that we brought to it a touch of our own recollected life.

May I add one detail, in itself trivial, but that you would grasp the importance of if you stayed a few months here?

None of our workers caused any trouble throughout the entire summer: there were no quarrels, there was no drunkenness, no one malingered when the work was hardest, and nobody got injured on one of the farm machines. This had never happened before in living memory. This labor force from outside the community is essential today when vocations to manual work have become infrequent. At that time such reinforcements did not seem to be absolutely necessary, but it was a tradition that La Trappe should provide work in an area that was far from rich. So we found jobs on the farm, as best we could, for a dozen or so workers who had previously been employed in the chocolate factory. They were rather a rough lot, difficult to manage, not very skilled, and there was often trouble with them. In serious cases we called on the only monk who knew how to impress the lay workers: Brother Sébastien, the giant with the fiery red beard who could tell them off in silence.

Most of them came from families that were indifferent and sometimes hostile toward religion. Indifference and hostility are not uncommon in the area around monasteries. Some see this as the devil's revenge. More prosaically I think these attitudes hark back to a period when the abbots were the feudal lords of the region. The only parts of France—Le Perche is among them—where farmers have become Freemasons are those where most of the land used to be owned by the monks. The peasants acquired the land at the Revolution as national property and are still afraid, centuries later, that if the church became powerful again it would confiscate their lands. Despite all this the three months of that summer were a time of honeymoon between workers and monks.

In this atmosphere Cosmas had slipped back into the noviceship without any difficulty. He was sustained by the peace and the joy that enfolded him. He made his own contribution as well. The discipline and the random contacts with the world that had previously irked him seemed no longer to be a problem. He had been assigned another cubicle in the dormitory, less noisy than Denys's Ear, where he had spent so many sleepless nights. Intellectually and emotionally he no longer made a rigid distinction between the time of prayer and other monastic activities. At the start of his noviceship he had astonished me by the speed with which he had picked up the gestures, attitudes, and style of a formed religious; now he astonished me again at the way he overcame his earlier difficulties, so much so that one might have thought that they had never existed. He shared with zest and apparently with relish in every aspect of community life. It so happened that the work I gave him at that particular time was pretty varied and had the added attraction of being rather unusual. He was one of those put in charge of the canvas village that formed a temporary addition to the guesthouse. I could see that he was busy, conscientious, and thoroughly happy as he led the new arrivals to the campsite; saw that they had blankets, sleeping bags, and storm lanterns; and at the first light of dawn went from tent to tent with a bucket of steaming coffee that he ladled out to the guests.

The only slightly disturbing thing was his extreme conscientiousness and his desire to be regarded as a model novice. His friend Dominique used to make friendly but hard-hitting jokes about this. Dominique had somehow discovered in the library some advice of St. Ignatius to his sons. He had been struck by one phrase that he alternated with his usual nicknames of God's goody-goody and Archangel Novice: he used to say to Cosmas in a would-be sententious manner, "Beware of unintelligent zeal!"

The time when the other two novices were to take their temporary vows was drawing near; I devoted most of my time to them and, as a result, rather neglected Cosmas. The few conversations that I had with him during that period confirmed my view that he had mastered his crisis and found his feet again. However, I was afraid that he might feel upset or neglected at being out of step with his two companions. But it didn't seem to worry him. Far from being slightly envious of Brother Jacques Marie and Brother Louis, which would have been understandable, he showed them ever more deference as their vows drew near: in their presence he seemed to fade into the background and would rush to pick up things they dropped or try to anticipate their every need.

In fact during these few weeks Dominique was his constant companion and probably had more influence in some ways than I had myself. I'm sure he had a good influence on him: a young man from outside the community, a friend and a contemporary, could afford to push Cosmas harder than I would have dared or even known how to. He had the art of chivying him gently along and of making fun of his intense seriousness, but without ever wounding him. This was a period in which Cosmas became more balanced, and to a great extent he had Dominique to thank for it.

Meanwhile my thoughts, feelings, and prayers were bound up with my two other novices as the day fixed for their temporary vows came still closer: before the whole community gathered in the chapter house they were about to complete the last stage of their initiation into religious life, and then, three years later, they would take their final and solemn vows of profession in the choir of the church and thus be irrevocably committed to the service of God according to St. Benedict's Rule and under the authority of the abbot.

The evening before they copied out the splendid formula in which they agreed to take the three vows of stability or attachment to the abbey, conversion of life, and obedience. Contrary to popular belief, the vows of poverty and chastity are not explicitly taken, though they are included in the vow of obedience: how could we sacrifice our own will unless we also renounced at the same time the demands of the flesh and the enjoyment of the goods of this world?

The detailed ordering of our ceremonies is a fascinating aspect of religious life, and far from being blunted as the years go by, they grow on one. The more we repeat the same words and gestures, the more they become natural and almost automatic—the more we discover their profound inner meaning, just as a pianist who practices daily no longer has any technical problems and can give himself entirely, heart and soul, to the task of re-creating the composer's emotion. Once more the chapter room was the scene of the age-old rite. Brother Jacques Marie and Brother Louis processed slowly through the two rows of monks in their choir stalls and moved toward Father Abbot and his assessors. Watched attentively by the fraternal community they were now committing themselves to more firmly, they exchanged the novice's habit for the habit of the professed monk, and put on the broad-sleeved habit, the black scapular, and the leather belt, and then they signed before Father Abbot the profession of faith they had copied out the previous evening, which was now formally accepted. Novice master that I was, these actions marked the end of a stage and they led me to examine my conscience. I had been responsible for these men for more than two years: had I prepared them as I should to stand on their own feet? Without claiming any credit for it, I believed that they would both contribute something to the community and would not cause any problems. Both of them still had the characteristics they had when they came to La Trappe. But one could also say that each had learned from the example of the other: Brother Jacques Marie's toughness was now combined with flexibility, and Brother Louis had caught something of Jacques Marie's precision and strength.

Yet part of my mind and heart was still preoccupied with Cosmas. I feared that this profession of faith would be an emotional occasion for him, since it would have been the day of his own vows if it had not been for the crisis which led Father Abbot to send him away for his trial period. Several times during the ceremony I couldn't help a sidelong glance to see how he was reacting. He seemed to be following everything with the intensity he brought to all our prayers and offices. But he didn't seem to be in the least disturbed and there was nothing for me to worry about.

As the newly professed monks came out of the chapter room, they did something that was not foreseen in the rite but that came spontaneously from the heart. First Brother Louis and then, following his example, Brother Jacques Marie embraced Cosmas at length: it was both an invitation to join them soon and a pledge that he, Cosmas, would forever be their privileged brother and their contemporary in religious life.

10

Autumn came round again, but with less splendor than usual. Each morning we woke up to find a thick mist clinging to the hillsides. There it remained throughout the day until by evening it filled the valleys with a sad, opaque silence. Dominique had gone back to his agricultural college. Our farmworkers were quarreling again. After all the bustle of the summer, the community went back to the winter rhythm of work and prayer, not without a certain regret. We are trained to avoid both a sauntering pace and a rushed one, but in our comings and goings one could detect a slowing down, a hesitation. Less time was spent in the fields: for the professed this meant longer hours of study and for the lay brothers more time spent in the workshops. At Matins the church was no longer illumined by the promise of dawn; the mist creeping in from outside turned the lamps to yellow; little clouds of condensation formed above our heads as we breathed; shaky voices struggled to reach the vaulted roof. A damp cold got through our clothes.

This atmosphere led to a certain amount of daydreaming, a temptation that I combated by concentrating on the tasks in hand. But I couldn't help feeling that a mood of gloom was slowly infiltrating the community. I felt it in myself, and I suspected it in others—notably in Cosmas.

The vows taken by his two companions meant that he was now alone in the novitiate. In the last few months, three candidates had applied and there were two more in the week that followed the temporary vows of Brother Louis and Brother Jacques Marie. But Father Abbot and I had refused them without too much difficulty. Four of them had not thought deeply enough about what monastic life involved and their vocations needed time to come to maturity; the fifth was an agreeable and enthusiastic young man, but his temperament made him obviously unsuitable for monastic life.

I've heard that some novice masters are very happy to work with just one novice. They try to turn him into their well-beloved son in the Lord, the disciple in whom their spiritual heritage can take root and grow, or as someone who can realize the ideal they have themselves failed to achieve. That is not my way of looking at it. I've always felt uneasy in those fortunately rare periods when I've only had one novice to look after. I believe that the formation of future monks is more a matter of preparing them to lead a community life than an exercise in individualistic spiritual education. This is easy enough to realize when the novices form a small group, but it is much more difficult to conduct on a one-to-one basis when the novice master is cut off from his novice by ten years' or more experience of religious life and when he has full authority over him: this is not the best way to get used to common life.

I'll put it even more strongly: whenever I had a group of novices to deal with, my personal relationship with each of them was deeper and more genuine. This was confirmed by my experience with Cosmas. Our almost daily conversations took place in an atmosphere of trust, but they seemed to lack an essential dimension. Did Cosmas himself feel a certain awkwardness at being my only partner in these conversations? It sometimes seemed that he was less open and confiding than when Brother Jacques Marie and Brother Louis were his constant companions. Rightly or wrongly I imagined that he was getting paler day by day; but I thought he was merely losing his summer tan.

I spoke to him on a number of occasions about this, suggested that he looked rather sad and worried, and urged him to let me know if anything was wrong. Once or twice I pressed the point more strongly and reminded him of the mistake he made before his breakdown, when he had failed to tell me about his problems. But he smiled and merely said: "No, Father, there's nothing wrong. I may be a little tired."

Cosmas's isolation had another effect. It meant that I had to assign him to other brothers for his work period. He told me what he would like to do: he wanted to be assistant sacristan and in charge of the flower arrangements. But the Cistercian vocation doesn't give much scope for this. There are no vases of flowers where we meet or pray or on our altars. However, all the year round we do lovingly place flowers before the statue of Our Lady, to whom all Cistercian churches are dedicated, and before the statue of St. Thérèse of Lisieux, who came from our own diocese of Sées. Cosmas had also revealed that he had long been fond of gardening. From the age of five or six until he went away for his military service he had looked after his own flower bed.

Unlike some other religious orders who go in for—or used to go in for—systematic mortification, it was never our custom to frustrate natural inclinations or, still worse, to assign novices or young religious to the work for which they felt the greatest repugnance. Yet I couldn't overlook the fact that Cosmas's first breakdown had been caused by too exclusive a concentration on prayer in choir and by his thoroughly un-Cistercian contempt for work on the farm. It didn't seem very sensible to give him work which of necessity would keep him in the church even outside the time of Divine Office.

I thought that I could half satisfy him by putting him to work with Brother Isidore, one of the few "natives" in the community—I mean simply that he came from Le Perche itself. Though we live here, it provides us with so few novices.

Brother Isidore was the son and grandson of market gardeners. With his beaked nose, sensitive face, and body as tough as a tree trunk in winter, he ruled over the vegetables, fruits, and flowers. But the needs of the community forced me to modify this plan. The extra work on the silo, the lack of communication between Father Secretary and Brother Augustin, who was in charge of the farm, and the incompetence of another brother meant that the abbey accounts were full of mistakes and omissions and needed to be straightened out. Cosmas was the only person competent and available to provide the help that Father Secretary so badly needed.

When I told Cosmas about this new assignment, he looked alarmed and incredulous. I confirmed with a nod that the decision had been taken. He bowed, murmured "Very well, Father," and withdrew.

An hour later he asked to see me. He was shattered. Not so much out of disappointment at not getting the office he had wanted, but at the idea of spending long hours, day after day, checking the bills, making sure that the totals were added up correctly, ticking off checkbooks. He kept on saying: "Do you really think, Father, that this sort of work suits me?"

I replied by pointing out that this was a short-term task that would be over once the accounts were in order. I added that despite his rather frosty appearance, Father Secretary was really very warmhearted. He replied that he knew that. Then

I gently lectured him: "Do I have to remind you yet again, my son, of the equal value of work done according to the Rule and the orders of superiors, whether it is a matter of prayer or looking after the cattle or keeping accounts? And since this work has to be done by someone, by what right do you imagine that it is unworthy of you and more suitable for someone else? When will you understand that the evaluation of the work we do depends on the Lord, and not on our own judgment?"

I tried to keep the tone light, as if I could not take Cosmas's objections very seriously. But he was in no mood to appreciate my bantering tone. He tried to explain. He had perfectly well grasped and admitted the importance of work in our lives: he thought that he had demonstrated this since his return—and I agreed; he was ready to tackle with joy any material task assigned to him, even the most repugnant.

"But you must understand," he said, "that these money matters on which I'm supposed to spend my time for weeks and months cannot be reconciled with my ideal of religious life. Do you understand, Father?"

When he quoted the Gospels on the impossibility of serving both God and Mammon, I merely smiled. But I became angry when he said in conclusion: "Is it not possible, Father, that this chalice should pass from me?" To drag the sufferings of Christ into such petty affairs was scandalous!

This telling-off seemed to make him less strained. He settled down to work the next day and very soon Father Secretary told me how much he appreciated Cosmas's help. But the work was only half completed when suddenly one morning Cosmas came along and begged me to give him some other task. I realized that he had never fully accepted the work he had been assigned, and that the cup of his repugnance had gradually filled up, drop by drop, day by day, until it now overflowed. I was reluctant to talk in terms of duty and obedience. I gave way to Cosmas for fear of another breakdown. Father Abbot consented, but his skepticism about Cosmas's aptitude for religious life was confirmed. I apologized to Father Secretary for depriving him of this help. Cosmas was now to work under Brother Isidore in the garden.

I would have perhaps agreed to Cosmas's request less readily, were there not other reasons that made me afraid that he was once more about to meet with serious difficulties.

After the gloomy and misty start to autumn the community had to undergo a few weeks of strain, and no doubt in this way we atoned for the remarkable and too-easy happiness we had enjoyed during the previous two months. A certain amount of disorder began to creep into the life of the abbey. Some brothers were guilty of notable breaches of the rule of silence, either out of curiosity or an impatience they could not control; others were late for Divine Office, and there was general carelessness in the carrying out of community tasks.

It so happened that Cosmas was present at two incidents: the first—as you will see—was harmless enough, while the second was rather unusual. I was disturbed to see how he reacted on both occasions, as though he had still not understood what monastic life really is.

Monks remain human beings. They have to be men of passion; otherwise they could never commit themselves irrevocably to so single-hearted an adventure. You yourself once said to me that you came here to observe men in love with the absolute. They have chosen to live in the sight of God, whose gaze is both demanding and merciful. His unvarying light shows up the smallest faults, but in his goodness he offers boundless and unconditional forgiveness to all those who feel the need to be forgiven. Seen in this spiritual light, no imperfection is indifferent; but neither is it a cause for worry, provided it is seen as evidence of our weakness and does not lead to discouragement, revolt, or complacency. To fall somewhere along the road belongs to the human condition: but the monk, because of the exclusive commitment he has made to the Lord, is especially bound to pick himself up and resume the onward journey, indefatigably.

Of course, repeated faults can be a disturbing signal that reveals or heralds weariness, resignation, or, in extreme cases, a weakening in the spirit of obedience. Dom Philippe well understood what was happening: he reacted strongly and swiftly to the crisis that swept through the community, and the newfound gentleness we had noticed in him during the summer months did not stand in the way of his sense of duty.

But, on the other hand, to suppose that the presence of such faults calls into question one's whole conception of religious life merely proves that one has not understood it. That was, alas, Cosmas's reaction to the two incidents that he had the misfortune to witness.

One morning his work on the accounts led him to pay an unannounced visit to the kitchen. There he came across a brother, half hidden by the door of the stock cupboard, who was eating a bar of chocolate that would have topped off the rice pudding. Cosmas was horrified but he said nothing. But a few days later he happened to discover the same brother who, thinking he was unobserved in a remote corner of the piggery, took another bar of chocolate out of his pocket and proceeded to eat it. Cosmas was scandalized beyond measure at the idea that a religious could steal something, however small, that belonged to the community. He told me what had happened, naturally without mentioning the name of the offender. He was astonished when I named him straightaway. The whole community knew that this brother, whose piety was profound and who in other respects was scrupulous, had never been able to rid himself of a morbid passion for chocolate. He had frequently accused himself of this fault in chapter, but the most varied punishments had so far failed to cure him. Father Abbot had recommended in a fatherly way that if possible this brother should not work in the kitchen on days when the menu included this tempting product. His advice must have been forgotten that week . . .

As I spoke, I realized that now it was my own attitude rather than that of the chocolate stealer that scandalized Cosmas. His idealism and youthful intransigence could not accept the lighthearted way in which I described the lapses of our brother. So I changed my tone and reminded Cosmas of the weaknesses of the flesh.

"If La Trappe were made up only of sinless brothers," I said, "there wouldn't be very many left here."

I urged him to have compassion on a religious who was humiliated by committing such a notorious fault. I stressed the lesson in charity provided by Father Abbot, who, despite his customary strictness, had advised the guilty monk to avoid the occasions of temptation. And I suggested that he make an act of humility and pray that he would never have to repent of more serious faults.

I observed him as I spoke, and his look and attitude were perfectly clear: for him it was a staggering revelation that an abbey should contain such petty weaknesses.

The second incident was much more serious. One evening Father Secretary sent Cosmas to consult Brother Augustin on some point of detail. As he approached the farm buildings, he heard what sounded like bellowing cries, and looking up he saw framed in the lighted window and outlined against the white wall like a shadow play a scene which left him dumbfounded: the bearded Brother Sébastien, so tall and strong, was holding the thin and weak Brother Augustin by the shoulders, shaking him vigorously, and shouting at the top of his voice. Cosmas couldn't make out exactly what was being said, but it was obvious that abuse and insults were flying through the air. And on this occasion Brother Sébastien's complaints were certainly not silent.

When calm was restored we discovered that the quarrel was something to do with tractors. Brother Augustin had ordered a lay brother to use a tractor on which Brother Sébastien was doing some intricate repair work. The sudden starting of the engine had ruined all the work he had so carefully done and could have led to serious damage . . . though in fact it didn't. But Brother Sébastien cherished his machines with a violent and jealous passion.

When Cosmas managed to drag himself away from this—for him—incredible sight, he had rushed into my office and, wide-eyed, had murmured so softly that I had to ask him to repeat what he had said: "Brother Sébastien and Brother Augustin are fighting."

The next morning at chapter, after the office of prime and Father Abbot's commentary on an extract from the Rule, the abbot said: "Let us speak of our order."

Brother Sébastien and Brother Augustin prostrated themselves in their places and, at Father Abbot's invitation, they came one after the other and bowed down before him to confess their faults.

In his booming voice Brother Sébastien confessed that he had given way to an impulse of anger, which had led to violence in word and action. Always the professional, he couldn't help adding as an aggravating circumstance that his anger was particularly unjustified because anyhow the use of the tractor had not led to any serious damage.

But Brother Augustin claimed a large share of responsibility for the incident. He had stepped out of line and committed a sin of presumption by giving the order to use the tractor himself, instead of asking permission from Brother Sébastien, who was solely responsible for the farm machinery.

Brother Sébastien was reprimanded by Father Abbot, but the severity of his tone could not conceal—or so I thought—a touch of sympathy: of passionate temperament himself, held in check only by extraordinary self-mastery, he knew how difficult it must be for Brother Sébastien to overcome his violent nature. He ordered him as a punishment to beg his food in the refectory for a week. Brother Augustin's penance was to prostrate himself at the entrance to the church before the midday meal for three successive days.

I've already mentioned that there was still at that date a distinction between choir monks and lay brothers. Cosmas, as a choir novice, had been present at the chapter and heard the penances imposed on the two men. As we came out of the church for the next three days, he could see Brother Augustin prostrate on the ground—a posture that made him seem thinner than ever. And he saw Brother Sébastien kneel down before the superior and then before a dozen or so of the monks. They each put a few spoonfuls of their daily ration into the bowl he held out to them.

I tried to get Cosmas to talk about the whole affair. Whatever his feelings were, he should not keep them to himself and brood over them.

He had been deeply upset by the quarrel. He was equally upset by the penances inflicted upon the two brothers, the first serious penances in his time in the abbey. That a monk within the walls of his abbey should lose his temper in the way Brother Sébastien had was more a matter of astonishment than blame. But the penances imposed by Father Abbot seemed to him inhuman and too humiliating. I tried to put things in perspective. I said to Cosmas: "There can be no doubt that God loves people like Brother Sébastien who are generous, intransigent, and sometimes impulsive. He loves them as our Lord loved

St. Peter, not despite but through all his outbursts, his impetuous love, his denials, and his fears. But so serious and public a fault against silence, patience, and charity, two brothers fighting each other while other monks and a few mocking farmworkers looked on—this called for a serious punishment."

I added: "Indeed, I would have expected a more severe punishment, at least for Brother Sébastien."

Finally I expressed the hope that such incidents might help Cosmas to understand that religious life and the pursuit of perfection involved a number of difficult stages. But I knew that he was still dreaming of a community that would have neither serious faults nor heavy punishments.

11

By God's grace the violent clash between Brother Augustin and Brother Sébastien brought the weeks of stress to an end. Under the firm rule of the abbot, community life settled down again, like a flooded river resuming its ordinary course. More than that: the principle of compensation that meant that we had a troubled autumn after a blessed summer, once more worked in our favor. After a period of difficulty we always feel the need for peace, brotherly unity, and a devotion that is more fervent and yet more recollected and interior. There were discreet hints that an outside observer would not even have noticed, but to which we were sensitive: a way of smiling or exchanging a glance, a more sustained attempt to blend our voices together into a single voice during the recitation or singing of the Divine Office.

In this atmosphere of rediscovered calm, I tried to think straight about Cosmas and to help him to do the same so that he could sum up his progress. We talked every day for half to three-quarters of an hour. In consultation with Father Emmanuel, his spiritual director, I had drawn up a program of conversations intended to cover systematically every aspect of religious life from private prayer to life in community, from the Divine Office to manual work, from his physical state to the inner movements of his soul. When it happened—too rarely in my judgment—that Cosmas did not simply answer my questions but took the initiative in talking about what was on his mind, I was more than happy to follow wherever he led me.

He said that he was content with his lot: the work in the garden suited him and seemed to have a tranquilizing effect. He continued to work away at his studies just as he had done from the beginning: without being drawn to intellectual speculation, he studied conscientiously and showed a reasonable ability to assimilate knowledge and reflect upon it. He still had a clear preference for being in church for the Divine Office, though he no longer had the almost ecstatic fervor that he had enjoyed when he first came to La Trappe. The private prayers and devotions that he had originally been inclined to overdo now took up a reasonable amount of time: they were no longer excessive. Likewise his spiritual life seemed to be progressing in a balanced way. He no longer had the radiant look of complete happiness that one had seen in him in the first months of his novitiate after he had taken the habit. But one could not call him sad, and the change could be interpreted as evidence of greater maturity. And although as I've said his position as the only novice meant that he was to some extent a solitary in the community, all the fathers and brothers he had dealings with appreciated his deference, his kindness, and his eagerness to please. He was always on hand for small services, ever ready to volunteer for extra tasks and to make himself useful.

Anyone ignorant of the difficulties Cosmas had gone through would have seen in him what I saw in the first months he spent among us: a young religious with no problems. But I who had followed him stage by stage knew that his development was not wholly satisfactory.

True, Cosmas had experienced, repeatedly, a number of psychological shocks; but none of them had plunged him into the abyss of distress that had previously led us to dismiss him from the abbey. But had he merely managed to overcome them by calling on his reserves of energy, by using his powers of self-control that, perhaps, were about to give out? Or had he really developed deep down, and was he growing into a better and more solidly balanced personality and gaining a more accurate insight into realities?

Unfortunately it seemed that Cosmas had not radically corrected the errors of judgment under which he labored. One piece of evidence was his exaggerated repugnance for accountancy work. Another was the almost childish astonishment caused by the weaknesses and violence of certain of the brethren.

A phrase used by Dominique during his stay on the farm the previous summer kept coming back to me. We had talked about Cosmas on a number of occasions. He liked Cosmas and understood him, and although an unbeliever, was fascinated by the mystery of a religious vocation. One day when we had been working together shifting logs in the forest we call La Vente du Parc, he accompanied me on the walk back and discussed Cosmas at some length.

Suddenly he had paused, and in his characteristic way screwed up his mouth and looked upward as though following the flight of a bird; and then with his features restored to normal, he looked at me and said: "Cosmas's problem is not the abbey—it's himself."

Of course, that can be said of every one of us: it is always within ourselves that we find the cause and the solution to our problems. But it can happen that objective factors outside ourselves make our problems more or less insoluble: some professions are hedged about with conditions that exclude those who are perfectly capable of other work. What Dominique meant— and as the months went by, I was more and more afraid that he was right—was that Cosmas's difficulties of adaptation were not due to religious life itself and that, given his temperament, he would have had the same problems in any walk of life.

Cosmas was one of those who are the most vulnerable and demanding, the most sympathetic and the most awkward, whom one can't help loving and yet who are so difficult to help: he was led on by his sensitivity and dreams, like a child in the dark walking with arms outstretched. But that doesn't stop the child colliding with the corner of the table or the chest of drawers. Cosmas and his kind are not safeguarded from the bruises of life by their sensitivity or their dreams. They see life in the light of their own expectations, and through the mist that they think they can penetrate they see things as they ought to be. But the light cast before them is like that of a headlamp projected into a fog: the light is reflected back and it dazzles and blinds them instead of illuminating the darkness. They usually have lively minds; but their intelligence does not forewarn them of coming dangers or threats; it merely enables them to explain with hindsight to themselves or others what has happened. But such insights, however enlightening, do not make any lasting difference to them, for their dreams return as before.

If things and people correspond to their vision of the world, this type of character can become a great artist or a man of action. But if the world does not match their dream, then these same men can become hurt and wounded failures. When everything tends to confirm their inner hopes—or when they think that is happening—they impress one with a sense of effortless ease, of balance and unshakable conviction, arrived at, it seems, almost by accident. But once they become aware of the gap between their aspirations and reality, they can so easily fall into hopeless sadness, which they invariably make worse by a sort of mad logic. You remember the experiment we had to do in the physics class? The iron filings would speed across the paper and gather at the point where the magnet was concealed on the other side—and all the tiny specks of iron would lie parallel to the magnetic field. In a similar way, when the ever-active sensitivity of this type of man is wounded, he will look around and scan the horizon like radar and straightaway facts, memories, and arguments will converge in patterns to justify his disappointment and deepen his despair.

One would like to help them to open their eyes so that their inner struggles can be seen in perspective. But one can do no more than pray for them and wait, with great gentleness, until they emerge from the other end of the tunnel into which they disappear and where no one can accompany them.

Yet the surprising thing is that they so often come out of the tunnel much sooner than expected, sooner than less sensitive people would. Those who are carried along by their inner vision have such strength of imagination that contact with reality, though it may damage them, does not break their heart. When in the grip of despair, it is as though they have crossed a threshold (the same happens to those who are given to violence), which means that they are no longer in control of themselves; but then, the crisis over, they recross the threshold and as peace returns the vision takes shape once again. The calm lucidity and optimism they then experience are still more surprising.

In their relationships with other people they are both terribly dependent and terribly demanding. They are dominating, and yet in need of reassurance; they are emotional and dependent on other people—but other people they have refashioned according to their vision and their dream.

It is not difficult to understand why such characters should be drawn to adopt extreme positions and why, in particular, they should want to embrace the monastic life; but one can also understand why they should find it so difficult to adapt to that life when they are—or believe they are—called to it by the Lord.

A life wholly dedicated to God, without halfheartedness or compromise, fulfills their deepest desire for the absolute. They find reassurance in the silence of the enclosure and a life lived according to the Rule and obedience to superiors with every detail minutely covered. These things act as a sort of protective handrail or parapet. Cosmas had admitted, without any prompting from me, that his vocation contained an element of what he called cowardice.

Such idealists—or visionaries?—imagine that a religious house will provide the support they need among a group of sinless monks who live in an atmosphere of unalloyed holiness.

But then they wake up to the everyday reality. They discover a community of men who go about their work of serving God while remaining subject to ordinary limitations and material needs. In God's eyes they are men who have to come to terms with weakness, imperfections, and the tyranny of habit; for holiness is not a state in which one can settle down comfortably, but rather a distant goal toward which, day by day, they inch forward with humility and constant effort—rather like the mountaineer whose upward progress is so slow, and whose every mistake is gravely punished.

All of us, especially the young, know how disillusioning contact with reality can be. But the value they set on their interior dream and the unyielding quality of their ideal mean that characters like Cosmas are particularly exposed to this kind of disappointment.

In the last few years I had twice to deal with novices who had a similar kind of temperament—though, I must say, much less markedly than Cosmas—and I am glad to say that in both cases I was able to bring them gradually to work free from their illusions. It is indeed a matter of being set free, of being liberated: for though they are full of goodwill, they are at the same time captive souls, prisoners of the idea they have formed of religious life, and also prisoners of their own logic and of the expectations they have of others.

They need disillusionment without despair. They have to learn that they will not find in monastic life and its Rule a ready-made peace and perfection, but that monastic life and the Rule are rather a road toward peace and perfection that each one has to take at his own pace. They have to learn to accept and to love their neighbor as he is, knowing that the help and example of other people will inevitably and to some extent be flawed and disappointing; and that everyone has to find his own original way forward, which will depend on his personal relationship with God rather than the imitation of someone else.

Two things must happen simultaneously: they have to learn to see others and situations as they really are and to regain a sense of their responsibility for their own fate—and that is something more than goodwill, which implies a docile willingness to accept the advice they are given. Cosmas had both these characteristics, but they were offset by a marked tendency to take refuge in established convictions, even when they were false. There can be no doubt that he was still influenced by childhood memories: he had a sense of being let down by the discovery of his father's excesses and the decline of his mother into neurotic bigotry, and his brother's abrupt departure had seemed to him a betrayal. He had come through the desert of adolescence with his eyes fixed on the ideal vision of La Trappe, which he had glimpsed like a mirage on the horizon.

My task was to unseal his eyes; his was to have enough strength to let this happen. He was probably not responsible for his mistaken judgments; but perhaps he was responsible for the weakness he showed at the point where he emerged from the dream and had to face up to reality.

The most difficult problem for me was that of timing the stages of Cosmas's development. I didn't dare rush him, knowing how carefully sleepwalkers should be woken up. But I also felt guilty when he seemed to be getting nowhere, fearful as I was of failing to coax along the only novice in my charge at a brisk enough pace. I daily entrusted my worries to the Lord and implored his enlightenment. I consulted frequently with Father Emmanuel, Cosmas's spiritual director. Should one take the prudent course, all too prudent, no doubt? Or should one force the pace and compel Cosmas to tear away the veil that was concealing from him the transformed view of religious life that God expected of him?

Above all I was afraid that some new incident, over and above those that he had coped with so badly, would affect his already uncertain balance. Sometimes a boxer learns how to take blows without harm—and the more he receives, the less is he harmed; but when the body is not used to such treatment, the hail of blows can create such weakness that a fresh shock, even of a mild kind, can cause a collapse.

12

But Cosmas was to surprise me yet again. I was afraid that another incident or a shock would bring about another crisis. But he came to see me without any special reason and with no particular incident in mind; yet I found him in a worse state than I had expected.

The day before we had talked about his reading, and I had wanted to alter the emphasis somewhat so as to bring out more the importance of developing willpower. Cosmas seemed to be in low spirits and in a dull mood, but I didn't bother too much about that: he never got excited about intellectual work.

He asked to see me in the afternoon, adding that the conversation might well be rather lengthy. He arrived in my office at the appointed time and looked outwardly very calm, and this made his opening remark even more bewildering: "I've been thinking and praying about this a great deal, Father. I think it would be sensible for me to leave La Trappe for a few months."

Surprised as I was, I tried to stay calm and asked, as though rather amused: "What's the matter?"

"Nothing," he said, "everything and nothing. It's just that I'm confused."

I had no need to ask him any questions. He began to speak and I knew that once he started to unpack his troubles he would not stop until he had told me everything. As usual, he spoke slowly, as though picking his way carefully. I closed my eyes and remembered what he had been like two years before when his first crisis broke. Now he was more in control of what he was saying, his tone was more even, less excitable, and his language was more restrained. Yet I had exactly the same feeling: it was as though blood were spurting from an open wound in rhythm with an overstrained heart.

As I listened I was praying for him from the depths of my being. He gave a detailed account of the causes of his distress. He began by recalling the different stages through which he had gone: his acceptance of the need for a balance between Divine Office and secular work; the way he had overcome the trials of the last few months. But now he seemed to be sinking, almost drowning, in monotony. Everything including the office and prayer seemed to have become a matter of boring routine.

He used the word several times, rather wearily: routine, routine . . . and then he paused and asked me to bless him before continuing: "You see, Father, the only person in the whole community who seems really to burn, to be caught by the fire of love, is Father Abbot, cold as he may appear. You know that I respect and love you as your child in Christ, but sometimes I feel . . . I can't help feeling—forgive me for saying this—that your attitude when you go to the church is that of a good civil servant setting off for his office."

I couldn't help raising a slightly quizzical eyebrow at this. Cosmas went on to make his point clear: "Everything you do, the way you walk, your posture, your tone of voice, make me think—wrongly, you'll say, but I can't get the idea out of my head—that singing psalms and reciting the office are largely the fulfillment of a duty."

He continued: "You are not the only one, Father. All the brothers give the same impression. It is almost as if a monk, who happens to give some hint of enthusiasm or devotion in the way he speaks or acts, immediately feels rather guilty and gets back as soon as possible to the routine that overlays everything here in the way that snow blots out footprints. Dominique used to accuse me of being God's goody-goody because I was full of excessive zeal and fervor; but now I've become just another hack of the liturgy. Even a few months ago I was still filled with feelings of generosity when I prayed. But now my whole object is to avoid distractions and to concentrate on the meaning of the words I'm using."

He was rather excited as he said this. Then he took a grip on himself as if to prove to me that what he was about to say was not the result of any sudden rush of blood but was a serious and prayer-inspired decision. He went on rather more calmly: "I suppose you will say, Father, that these feelings are excessive and that I ought to be able to keep them in proportion. I know that perfectly well . . . But to do that I would have to get away from the atmosphere of the community for a time so that I could sort out my ideas somewhere other than at La Trappe. Even the most experienced divers need to come up to the surface occasionally so as to breathe fresh air."

Cosmas liked this image. He had used it several times.

But I found it disturbing. Up to a point I would have agreed with Cosmas if monastic life depended on surface impressions. It was true that a certain lassitude had been weighing the community down. Winter in Le Perche is slow to depart; it comes back again just when you think it gone. In March and sometimes even in April, there is a long and ambivalent time of waiting before spring finally arrives. The abbey buildings were still at that date unheated, and the end-of-winter cold, though it may have been less intense, was harder to bear. And Lent, which for us begins six months early in September, further diminishes our powers of resistance. Cosmas was not altogether wrong in thinking that the community was in a state of torpor that resulted in routine and monotony. But so long as he remained dependent on superficial impressions—whether justified or not—he could not hope to arrive at a permanently balanced approach to religious life. For a monk truth is not a matter of feeling; it depends on perseverance and graces received.

A few days earlier I had been wondering whether or not I should force the issue and get Cosmas to face up to the realities of religious life. He had put my doubts at rest by asking to leave the abbey for the sake of his health. This provided a chance to burst the abscess even if it meant using the scalpel. The time had come.

I began by chiding Cosmas for not having mentioned his new problem earlier. He said that for many weeks he had hoped that his difficulties would go away of their own accord. He was afraid that he might alarm me unnecessarily by talking about them and give them more substance than they really had. I pointed out his mistake. The most important virtue in a novice was a trusting, childlike openness.

Then I reminded him how futile and even absurd it was to try to judge the value of prayer by one's feelings or outward effects. Did I have to refer him to the most basic teachings of the masters of the spiritual life? Did he need to relearn the rudiments of mystical experience? Had he forgotten that St. Thérèse of Lisieux found prayer arid right up to her dying moments, and that the church saw in this aridity one of the surest proofs of her heroic sanctity?

He heard me out, with eyes cast down. Then he looked up and said: "If it were merely a matter of my own dryness, Father, I would accept it. But that the whole community . . ."

This made me react with some passion: "What do you really know about the whole community? Have you forgotten that to live by the Rule and the orders of superiors, day in, day out, for a whole lifetime, is only possible where there is great love and passionate fidelity? Do you really think that obedience, as it should be lived by a monk, could be a heartless mechanical routine? Have you never heard the remark of the saintly Pope Pius X? He said that he would canonize on the spot, without summoning the devil's advocate, any boy who had kept the rules throughout his school days. And the pope was talking about a child."

Was Cosmas really so ignorant about the men he lived among and whom he had the gall to consider—I picked up his phrase—no better than routine civil servants stuck in their groove? Had he learned nothing from Brother Sébastien's violent outburst that he had witnessed a few months before? Although by God's grace the majority of monks were not converts and had led irreproachable lives, there were nearly always in every abbey a few who had had a turbulent life in the world. The life led by Charles de Foucault before his sudden conversion was typical of others before they answered God's call.

"It's no accident," I added, "that a Trappist house should include a certain number of these ardent souls: you have to be madly in love with God to persevere throughout a whole lifetime with total abnegation."

But Cosmas should not imagine that the majority of monks, though they had not led tormented lives, could get by with any less heroism or love. To move from a conventional childhood and youth to the calm and irrevocable acceptance of obedience could be just as awesome a trial of strength as a dramatic swing from one extreme to another: it was like trying to climb a slope without any preliminary run-up.

I stressed this point: the absence of perceptible outward effects was in no way a proof of inadequate fervor; it could indeed be evidence of the highest degree of self-mastery—such as one finds in virtuosos or athletes. We are called "regulars," and this is because we live according to the Rule of our holy Father St. Benedict; but it could also be because we push "regularity" as far as our strength permits. And for that, too, something more than mediocre love is needed.

I sensed that a struggle was going on within Cosmas, and one could trace it in his changing facial expressions. The reasonable side of his nature understood and accepted what I had just said. But it was evidently no longer in control. One could say that all his inner demons were in league together to intensify and aggravate the pain that for the moment he needed like a drug.

He repeated what he had already said: "It's better that I should go away . . . go away for a time."

I asked him what difference going away would make to his basic problem. Then he began to speak with great urgency, as though pleading with me.

He reminded me how valuable his first departure from the noviceship had been. He would always remain grateful to Father Abbot and to me for insisting on him leaving. If he had stayed at La Trappe, if he had not stood back from the life here, he would not have gotten over his difficulties so quickly, or perhaps never have gotten over them at all. He added with great humility: "I know that it's not a very heroic solution and that someone stronger than me could overcome the crisis while remaining here. But I know the limits of my strength and I know how to take a proper grip on myself. The method that worked last time will work just as well this time—it simply must."

He had already devised a plan that was strangely similar to the one he had worked out for his first absence from the abbey. And as I listened it came home to me how readily this kind of temperament indulges in psychological and emotional pilgrimages and returns to the people, places, and methods that have been helpful in the past.

I didn't know whether to smile or be outraged when he quoted in support of his decision the extract from the Rule of St. Benedict that had been read in chapter that very morning and that was concerned with runaway religious: "If any brother who through his own fault departs or is cast out of the monastery wishes to return, let him first promise entire amendment of the fault on account of which he left; and then let him be received back into the lowest rank, that thus his humility may be tried. Should he again depart, let him be taken back until the third time. But let him know that thereafter all opportunity to return will be denied to him."

The last time this text had been read, Dom Philippe briefly commented on it to bring out the preeminent value of the vow of stability that binds each monk not to the order in general but to a particular abbey, and he had emphasized that any departure not authorized by the superiors was a grave fault. His tone seemed to hint—or came close to hinting—that he thought our Father Benedict was excessively gentle toward such runaways.

But by contrast this time he followed the mainstream tradition that stressed God's exemplary patience and the patience that St. Benedict laid down should be used in dealing with such offenders. And yet Cosmas saw in the text an argument in favor of his plan for a second temporary departure from the abbey.

"My poor child," I said, "you're on a completely wrong track. St. Benedict didn't leave us a procedural code but a rule of life and, if possible, holiness. The recommendation to welcome back up to three times brothers who have left the monastery is—as you heard Father Abbot remind us this morning—a counsel of charity toward the offending monks. It's not a right they possess nor an obligation imposed on superiors, still less a way of enabling novices with problems to be gradually acclimatized to religious life."

I felt that my ironic tone, far from calming Cosmas down, was being used as a pretext to enable him to feel misunderstood and to plunge still more deeply into his distress. So I tried to speak in a way that would be more suited to his troubled state. Yet I was also determined to be firm on the principle at stake and wanted to forget about the blind alley down which he was heading.

With as much gentleness as I could summon—and God knows that my heart was filled with love for him and a desire to help him—I tried to make him see where his problem lay and what the solution was.

It was perfectly true that his first departure from the abbey, decided upon by Father Abbot after his breakdown, had turned out to be a wise move which had good results. But you cannot turn a saving intervention, a kind of surgical operation, into a regular means of treatment. In the course of his religious life every monk—and Cosmas perhaps more than others because of his ever-active sensitivity—was bound to encounter disappointments; but if he were going to leave La Trappe every time this happened, how could he truly claim the noble title of monk?

I attacked his last line of defense: "If you think that your present difficulties make your departure necessary, would you be able (but why? and how?) to assure us that other difficulties would not lead you (how many more times?) to ask permission to leave again in order, as you put it, to be able to breathe?"

He was much too honest to dodge the question or to give me an answer of which he could not be sure. His silence was a tacit admission that he was unable to make a guaranteed commitment. I felt admiration for the spiritual honesty of which he had just provided further evidence. But now the unambiguous conclusion had to be drawn. I went on: "You compare yourself to a diver who has to come up to the surface from time to time. But doesn't that merely prove that the sea is not his true element? When fish, whose natural environment is water, come up to the surface, they die of what we call fresh air. That is precisely the problem. What kind of creature are you, my child? Are you one of those who are attracted to religious life as the diver is drawn to the sea—from the outside? Or are you a monk who is made to live in it?"

Cosmas must have been half expecting this verdict. But he felt the blow all the same. I saw him hunch forward on the stool on which he was sitting, like a leather bottle that gradually collapses as the water is drunk; he slumped forward and I sensed that within him was being played out the mystery of a man wrestling with himself and with God.

I paused for a moment, hoping that silence and grace would calm him down and enable him to put some order into his thoughts. I prayed that the Holy Spirit might enlighten him . . .

I know, my friend, that this appeal to the Holy Spirit that you have so often heard from me, may seem to you to be an empty form of words. Even many believers find it difficult to understand the third person of the Trinity as a living reality. Perhaps only a man and a woman in whom dwells great love can be aware of this presence of a third, who is indefinable and yet more real than a being of flesh, who accompanies them everywhere and is their love. We who try to live constantly in the sight of God feel and know that there overflows from the infinite love of the Father and Son a presence and a power who dwells in the ground of our being and who is the Spirit of Love. His enlightenment springs from within our hearts, not like the midday sun which is the symbol of unfailing truth, but more like a light perceived in the midst of darkness. His light provides guidance on the way ahead without ever robbing us of our freedom.

So I prayed that the Holy Spirit would act within Cosmas and scatter the clouds that obscured a truthful vision of things and people.

I waited for quite a long time. When I thought that Cosmas was calm again and in a fit state—or so I thought—to profit from what I had to say, I spelled out the details. As a novice who had not taken any vows, Cosmas was perfectly free to leave the monastery. But if he did, there could be no question of granting him permission to return. He could either overcome his crisis with the help of prayer—his prayer and our prayer—and grace, and he should do so here and now. Or that was beyond his strength, in which case . . .

I paused, and he echoed my words: "In which case, Father?"

It was obvious from the trembling in his voice that he knew what the answer would be.

"In which case," I said, "it would be proved beyond doubt that your place is not in La Trappe. That wouldn't mean that you were not sincere in seeking admission to the abbey; nor would it mean that you would not be happy serving God in some other way. But it would prove that you were mistaken about yourself and your ability to lead the Cistercian life. And God in his infinite mercy has warned you of this while there is still time, before you had taken your temporary vows."

Cosmas looked neither surprised nor indignant nor rebellious. I noticed merely that when he looked at me his eyes seemed brighter and more piercing than usual.

"No, Father," he said calmly, "I can't agree with you. I've always had, and I still have more than ever, the absolute certainty that my place, willed by God, is here and nowhere else. It is the only thing I have never doubted even in troubled periods or when, as today, I feel the need to go away for a time."

He wanted to make this quite clear: "If there is any one point on which my conscience tells me that I should not submit to the judgment of others, *whoever they may be,* it is on this."

Once again it seemed wiser not to reply straightaway. I invited Cosmas to kneel down and kneeled down beside him. We said the Our Father, a decade of the rosary, and the Veni Creator, after which we had a few moments of silent prayer.

Then I told him to rise. I said that now he knew all the factors in the situation, he should pray earnestly to the Holy Spirit, who was the Spirit of counsel, wisdom, and strength.

"In a few days," I concluded, "when you feel calm and enlightened, you will make your decision. If you make up your mind to stay here, we will see in that decision a sign that you really are called to serve God within the walls of the abbey, and our only concern will be to help you in difficult times to overcome the weakness that afflicts us all. But if you persist in your belief that you must leave once again for a brief spell in order to breathe in some fresh air outside and then return, then it would be more sensible and honest to think in terms of a final departure."

Cosmas seemed unmoved, not even by the word *final.* It was almost as though he were already somewhere else, where my arguments no longer affected him or, worse still, where they could no longer reach him. However, I conceded that he had the right to one last remaining glimmer of hope: the decision of Father Abbot, whom I would consult right away.

Dom Philippe listened without surprise to my account of Cosmas's latest crisis. When I had finished, he made a point of not reminding me that from the start he had expressed doubts about Cosmas's ability to realize what he thought was his vocation. With eyes shut, he simply murmured, "Poor boy," and then slowly opened his eyes so that he could observe my response to his questions: "At first I thought he was unstable. Now it seems more likely that he is weak. Would you say so? And it's because of that that he finds it so difficult to cope when he is put out or disappointed."

Then he added after a pause for thought: "The only thing that worries me is the strength and constancy with which he claims to be so sure about his vocation . . . and to reject our opinion. That doesn't fit in with the hypothesis of weakness."

He looked at me again, and he must have read on my face that I was just as puzzled as he was by the contradictions in Cosmas's character. Then Dom Philippe shrugged his broad shoulders to indicate that there was nothing more he could do and, tapping his fingers on the desk—an unusual gesture for him—concluded: "In any case, Father, you are right. We can only disapprove of his idea of leaving. And if he insists on going, we will have to conclude that he doesn't belong here. I don't know whether I'll be any better at convincing him of this than you have been. But tell him to come to my office tomorrow morning after Matins."

I left Father Abbot and looked for Cosmas so that I could pass on this summons to him.

His choir stall was empty. His novice's habit, neatly folded, was on his bed in the dormitory. He had removed his lay clothes from the wardrobe, but he had not asked for his personal belongings, which were still in a drawer in Father Secretary's office. No one saw him leave. But next morning the little ironwork gate near the bullocks' stable, which gave directly onto the fields, lay open.

13

Cosmas's sudden departure meant that for the first time since I became novice master, I was temporarily unemployed and had no novices to look after. This state of affairs didn't last long, anyway, because Father Abbot had agreed to my suggestion that we should accept two more postulants, who were due to arrive at the abbey within a fortnight. They were about the same age—twenty-three or twenty-four—were vaguely related, and their shared childhood had developed into a mature and adult friendship. The intention of joining La Trappe had been a youthful secret between them. They got the idea after a cycle ride had brought them into these parts. It grew upon them. They were like two children who build a secret hut in the depths of the woods, to which they alone know the way, or so they imagine. In fact their families knew one another well, had discussed them more than they suspected, and had gotten used to the idea that they had a shared religious vocation. They had taken their decision together; and together they had confirmed it during a long retreat made here, at the end of which they told me of their plans: they wanted to enter La Trappe together as postulants. This had made me very happy for Cosmas, for he would no longer be alone in the novitiate. But I hadn't had time to tell him about the new arrivals.

Father Abbot agreed that I should use this unexpected break in my duties as novice master to make an eight-day retreat on my own.

It may seem odd that in a life that is already one long retreat, we should feel the need to pause and enter an atmosphere of even deeper recollection. But speaking generally, all professions recognize that everyday activities need to be balanced by periods of renewal and in-service training. While diocesan seminaries have fewer and fewer recruits, the word *seminar* has been revived, so it appears, among businessmen. The monastic profession is no exception. The very regularity of our life is a help, but it can also lead to the danger of routine and overfamiliarity. This is no imaginary threat, even if Cosmas saw it in an exaggerated and unjustifiable way. A few days in retreat allow us to see ourselves with lucidity and, if need be, to reshape our lives and to continue with still greater insight.

A novice master may feel the need for a retreat with extra urgency. Because his mind, heart, and prayer are constantly preoccupied with the difficulties of his novices, he may well find that his own problems are being neglected. I felt very strongly the need to break with the recent past in order to fulfill my duty toward the two postulants who would shortly be arriving. After the tense atmosphere that followed my confrontation with Cosmas and his second crisis, it seemed to me to be useful to cleanse and purify my own spiritual state. For I had now to look to the future that was embodied in these two young men; the Cosmas affair, alas, was over.

The way he had left us—he practically fled—was surely a sign that he was unsuited for the irrevocable commitment of religious life. His desire to serve God had been perfectly sincere. And it could have been satisfied by our Cistercian life if only he had been clear-sighted enough to understand it and had had the strength to take it as a whole, whatever the merits or the fragility of the men who tried to live it out. But he had neither the strength nor the lucidity to do so. God had not granted him these graces. And that was probably the heart of the matter: it seemed that on one essential level neither prayer nor grace brought any effective help to Cosmas, and so he was unable to overcome his crisis. More than anything else, this was evidence that his entry into La Trappe was a mistake.

And yet even during this time of retreat, my thoughts kept on coming back to Cosmas, in spite of myself and though I knew that they should not have done so.

The discovery that a postulant is not suited for monastic life is—after a first reaction of disappointment—usually accepted calmly as a restoration of order, a problem solved, and (why not put it bluntly?) a relief. But in Cosmas's case the word *failure* continued to haunt my thoughts. It was a failure for him, because he had never doubted his vocation, even on the day he fled La Trappe. A failure, too, perhaps, for the community that had not provided him with a vision of monastic life that could match up to his dreams. A failure and a lesson in humility for me, who had been mainly responsible before the Lord for his spiritual progress: it could be that someone else would have grasped earlier than I did the weaknesses and complexity of Cosmas's character, and so been able to protect him against himself and convince him that he was on the wrong track. But should one also speak of . . . God's failure? I mean simply this: did God want this man to enter his service as a reformed Cistercian in La Trappe? The answer seemed to be negative inasmuch as Cosmas had not received superabundantly the graces he needed. But I couldn't be sure of that. During the eight days of attentive recollection and fervent prayer, I couldn't help asking the Lord again and again: did you really want, and do you still want, Cosmas to be here, and want it with that special desire that makes a monk? Despite the long hours of peace and enlightenment that God in his grace granted me, I never felt that I received a straightforward answer to this question.

The two new postulants arrived as expected the week after I finished my retreat. I was reassured by their presence and consoled to feel that I was once more on home ground, in a familiar world. Cosmas had been a difficult novice: he surprised us at first by appearing not to have any problems, and then he embarrassed and discouraged us by the questions he raised. These two young men were different in appearance and attitude, but they were both ruggedly healthy and honest. They would have the ordinary difficulties of adaptation to religious life, and my previous experience as novice master would be once more relevant. There was something to get hold of—something that had been lacking in Cosmas. They might possibly have to deal with the obstacle of their remarkable friendship: I would have to help them to extend it gradually to embrace the whole community. But I was familiar enough with that problem, and knew how to deal with it.

As I reverted to familiar joys and worries, I began to forget about Cosmas. But not in my prayers: because I had been responsible for him, he will have a privileged place in my prayer life until the day I die. This he shares with all my former postulants and novices, whether or not they persevered in religious life. And Cosmas was assured of a special place in my prayer precisely because he could neither understand nor accept his failure.

But he had ceased to be an immediate cause of worry and reflection when, three months after his departure, I received a letter from him.

Was it because I was afraid that my newly found peace would be disturbed or the feeling that everything had been said and that the letter could add nothing new? Whatever the reason, my instinct was to put it in a drawer, unopened. But when another letter arrived a month later, a scruple began to worry me. I told Father Abbot about it. Dom Philippe slightly pursed his lips—on his immobile face, that was the equivalent of a smile.

"You astonish me, Father," he said. "Keeping sealed letters solves nothing. It doesn't make sense. Open them and read them. If we were wrong in our final decision about Cosmas, then his letters will reveal something—an unusual choice of words, a different tone—that will show whether God's action on him has been such as to lead us to reexamine his case. But if these letters merely confirm what we already know, you can destroy them."

I burned the first two letters of Cosmas after reading them. And the ones that came later.

In the first letter he began by apologizing for the suddenness of his departure. He justified it by his utter conviction that he needed to go away and by his almost physical fear of another confrontation with me, which would inevitably be painful and, in his eyes, useless. Apart from that the first letter and all the remaining ones were a rehearsal in another tone of the letters he had written two years previously. Cosmas—it was thoroughly in character—liked to go back in time and start again. He had deliberately chosen the same peaceful setting as after his first crisis so that he could think things over. He had taken refuge with the former teacher who had put him up before. He had been in touch with the parish priest of the village near Autun where he had worked for a few months as a lay helper. The old priest was not surprised to find that Cosmas had left La Trappe a second time and, sensing something amiss, had declined to take him on. By sheer obstinacy and writing around Cosmas had managed to join a parochial team working in a Paris suburb.

True, there were certain differences of form and tone between the two sets of letters: Cosmas was more mature, his judgments were more penetrating, and his views on people and situations were less black-and-white; the style was less peremptory; he was choosing his words more carefully and describing various incidents with more subtlety. But having noted these differences, one felt bound to raise the same questions as before. Was Cosmas really experiencing something new, or was he merely looking for confirmation of what he had already decided? Was he searching for the truth about his life or, this truth being determined in advance, was he seeking supporting arguments to consolidate it for himself and for others? Now that I knew Cosmas so much better, the answer was not in doubt: he had left us without the slightest hesitation about his eventual return to La Trappe. Wasn't that precisely what he had told me? After his first departure he had borrowed our jargon and agreed with us speaking of a "trial period." This time he avoided such language: he talking only of rising to the surface, getting his breath back, overcoming his crisis.

The conclusions of his letters followed logically from all this. Contact with other forms of life confirmed him daily in his vocation . . . The feelings of disappointment that had caused this second crisis had almost vanished . . . Now he felt surer than ever about his vocation . . . His return was merely a matter of a few weeks—just the time he needed to fulfill the engagements he had undertaken in his temporary parish—a scout camp and holiday camps with the children.

As the months went by, his letters became more natural in tone—almost relaxed. I don't know whether you have ever had to deal with this type. They really are astonishing. You see them bogged down in the most appalling difficulties that drive you almost to distraction; you torture yourself in mind and heart to discover some way of helping them. And then suddenly they come back to you as though nothing had happened. It is as though the stormy abyss in which they were plunged turns out in the end to be no more than a slightly choppy sea or an overhot bath.

Never in any of his letters did Cosmas mention the decision I passed on to him and that had the full backing of Father Abbot:

if he left us in the way he was proposing, his departure would be final. He made no mention of it at all, except in his very last letter, the only one I have kept. Here is how it ends:

> You must have been surprised, Father, that in all my letters I write as though my return to La Trappe were not in doubt. That is the truth: *I have no doubts about it.*
>
> Perhaps you will say that it is utterly presumptuous and unreasonable for someone seeking entry into religious life to want to sweep aside a decision of the novice master that has been approved by Father Abbot.
>
> I want you to understand, Father. I know that I left La Trappe in a highly unusual way. That may lead you to think that my vocation is not really serious. I think that would be a false conclusion. The fact is that I know my weakness—or rather my special kind of weakness. You see, Father, the only kind of courage I have—and always will have by the grace of God—is that of never abandoning my vocation, which is as strong today as it was when I arrived at the abbey. That apart, I know how weak I am; and I can imagine how self-deceptive and absurd my way of getting used to religious life must seem—going in and out like a bather who can't bring himself to dive once and for all into a freezing sea. Don't judge me, Father: I do my best, but I intend to answer the call that I still hear, with whatever strength I can summon . . .

He then explained that he had satisfied all his commitments and could therefore return very soon, probably in about a fortnight, in late October. The letter ended:

> I assure you, Father, that my soul and my conscience tell me that I have never ceased to belong to the community. I remained and remain your son. I will knock on your door and, humbly prostrate before you, ask for forgiveness and a blessing.

With great sadness in my heart and without really thinking about what I was doing, I crumpled up the letter and the envelope and flung them into the wastepaper basket. Cosmas was still doggedly determined to pursue his vocation; I had no doubts about his sincerity; but I still felt under no obligation to accept his idea of a monastery that one left after disappointments and to which one returned when one felt at peace with oneself.

But almost immediately the thought struck me that very soon Cosmas would present himself at the porter's lodge, that I would have to give clear instructions to Brother Porter, and that maybe even we might have to decide what to do should Cosmas get into La Trappe without telling anyone.

I took the letter out of the wastepaper basket, uncreased it as best I could, and went to seek advice from Father Abbot once again. A sad smile came over his face.

"Father," he said, "we can't refuse to welcome a man in trouble. See him and talk to him, but outside the enclosure so that he can't misinterpret the meaning of your action. May the spirit of God inspire you. Let me know when Cosmas arrives; if I'm free, I'll go to the church and pray for both of you. I can't make out whether he is perverse or persevering. This is a painful case, and a strange one."

I told Brother Porter not to let Cosmas into the abbey when he arrived, but to direct him to the guest chapel.

14

Cosmas appeared in the porter's lodge early one Sunday afternoon when he knew that I would be free to talk to him for a couple of hours. The door leading into the abbey was open to admit a group of visitors; Cosmas was about to go through when Brother Porter motioned him to stop. He gave four short rings on the bell, the signal we had arranged to warn me of Cosmas's arrival, and led him round the outside of the building to the guest chapel.

I found him there on his knees and head in hands. Before him in the main aisle was the small suitcase that is always brought by those who come here intending that this will be their last earthly journey. I kneeled down for a time on the other side of the aisle. I begged the Holy Spirit to enlighten my mind and, if need be, my decisions. I knew that at this very moment Father Abbot would be in the abbey church praying for the same intention.

When my mind was clear I got up and indicated to Cosmas that he should follow me. The sound of voices arising from the parlor made me give up the idea of taking him there, as I had intended. We went outside and I suggested that he should follow me along the path that leads down to the lakes.

Huge cotton-wool clouds, clearly defined, rolled above our heads as they do so often close to the sea. When they obscured the sun, one felt a certain nip in the air. But the earth had not yet lost its summer heat, and the autumn sun was still quite warm.

In this landscape that has known so many enchanted autumns, that year's splendor outstripped anything I could remember. The edge of the forest unfurled its long winding tapestry of red and gold along the smooth sinuous line of the hills. Fruit trees gleamed in the fields and the orchards. Motley leaves of green and bright yellow slowly tumbled down from the hedges onto the grassy lower slopes.

Traffic was brisk that Sunday afternoon. The track that joins La Trappe to the main road was not yet tarmacked, and the cars raised a cloud of dust that took some time to settle. It would have been difficult to talk properly, so we walked on in silence until we reached the path that follows the embankment of Lake Chaumont. We stopped at the sluice gate and Cosmas stood alongside me, one foot on the low brick parapet.

I looked at him, hoping that he would be able to join in my act of thanksgiving for so much beauty.

For some time we remained side by side, silent and full of wonder. The gold of the birch trees, the copper of the aspens and the red of the whitebeams, the yellow and orange of the elms and the brown of the oaks still streaked with green, the silky white of the clouds scudding across the limpid blue sky—all these colors were reflected in the lake with a remarkable clarity and gave it the dimensions of the sky. When the shadow of a cloud passed over the lake, it was more like a watercolor with fainter tints. Now and again a gust of wind rippled the surface, and then the reverse image of the trees trembled; and there was a fleeting splash of freshness and light as a tench or a perch leaped out of the water to swallow a hovering insect.

The silence was broken by passing cars. When we were alone again, I dragged myself away from this almost unreal spectacle, left the road, and set off into the woods beside the lake. I invited Cosmas to join me and said: "Well, my son?"

He repeated, often using the same language, what he had written in his letters. He was calm enough, and his steady voice was enriched by his Burgundy accent. He stressed what he had gained from this absence of a few months, not only for the present but for the future as well, and said that it had enabled him to enter a new and important stage in his acclimatization to monastic life.

"You may find it surprising," he said, "that I should have to leave the abbey the way I did in order to understand and accept what other postulants learn without ever leaving. I have to admit, Father, in all humility, that this makes me a mediocre novice and something of a nuisance. I'm not surprised that you and Father Abbot should have reached such gloomy conclusions about the genuineness of my vocation. But I'm certain, more certain than ever before, that it is the voice of the Lord that calls me back to the monastery."

He went on at some length along these lines, with great conviction and serenity. Just as in his last letter, he ended by asking for forgiveness, a blessing, and a welcome back.

We had reached the point where the wood narrows down between the road to Mortagne and the upper lake whose overflow ran this way. I crossed the road and led Cosmas along the bed of the stream to the bank of the upper lake. Rustic inns and pedal boats now shatter its peace, but at that time it was still charged with mystery. The lake was almost round, smaller than the lower lake, and surrounded by pines whose deep green dimmed the glowing autumn colors. The shadows had gradually reached water level. Cosmas followed me toward the sunny side of the lake where he sat down on the stump of a recently felled oak tree whose branches had not yet been lopped off.

I recollected myself for a final prayer. Cosmas waited, his eyes expressing an indefinable attitude made up of intensity, goodwill, and unshakable resolution. It was almost as though he were challenging me.

Should I try, quite simply, to show that one cannot seriously speak of a vocation that needs periods away from the abbey to be fulfilled? Or should I leave him a glimmer of hope, while making absolutely clear the conditions that would be attached to his eventual return? Without quite knowing why, I began to speak very slowly, using a voice that was not altogether natural to me and that was no doubt too solemn: "Cosmas, my son. Knowing in your soul and your conscience that the Lord is listening to you and that you will be accountable to him through all eternity for the answer you give, and supposing that we give you permission to return to La Trappe so as to live among us the monastic life according to the Rule of our Father Benedict and the holy reformers of the Cistercian family, are you sure—as far as you can be with the grace of God—that this time your return would be final?"

I had hardly pronounced my last word before Cosmas began to reply, using the same solemn tone and rhythm. It was as though his voice, though different from mine in timbre, somehow took over from mine so that question and answer came from the same source.

"Father," said the voice, "I can neither lie to you nor lie to myself nor lie to God . . . I cannot promise you that I will never have to undergo further crises and never to need another break in my initiation into religious life . . . But my vocation is unshakable. It comes from God, and in the full knowledge of what I am saying and undertaking, I beseech you to welcome me back among the brethren as a novice."

I wished now that I had not embarked on this conversation in so melodramatic a fashion. For the point was not to determine whether or not Cosmas would have to undergo further crises—there could be no doubt that he would—but rather to determine how he would come through them. The question raised by Father Abbot a year earlier came back to my mind: was Cosmas unstable or weak? If he were merely weak, we could guide and help him: when faced by fresh difficulties, he would simply have to undertake that he would make that act of confidence in God, in us, and in himself that he had been unable to make a few months ago; and that he would be ready to abide by our judgment, and not his, as to the best means of restoring his balance. But if on the other hand he was unstable, he would have to be made to understand that his temperament was incompatible with religious life, which is made up of constancy and regularity.

I tried to explain all this calmly. He interrupted me almost brutally: "My vocation is what it is, Father, and I know that I can face up to it, even though I have to begin all over again several times. I can't promise that I will never have to labor under further difficulties, but I am now sure that I can overcome them by leaving the abbey for a few months."

This complete misapprehension was hardly credible. I had to remind him yet again that this way of solving difficulties was wholly irreconcilable with the religious commitment of a Trappist. The genuineness of his vocation would have to be judged in the light of the following criterion: could he, yes or no, overcome future crises without having to leave La Trappe for a temporary period?

The question was clear enough, but Cosmas did not answer it. It was as though he didn't *want* to answer it, as though the whole matter was out of his hands.

He merely said—and I felt that he was addressing the Lord and calling upon him as a witness: "I want to try and answer God's call."

There was a pause. I couldn't say how long it lasted.

We were seated side by side on this fallen tree trunk, surrounded by the blazing glory of the forest, by this tranquil lake, and yet we were both involved in a reality beyond this world where our souls would be called upon to meet and understand each other better than we had so far managed to do.

I watched Cosmas intently: I no longer knew into what mysterious realms his thoughts, dreams, and prayer had strayed. How could someone who was neither proud nor mad nor wildly obstinate persevere in this kind of intermittent vocation?

I arose, looked him straight in the eyes, placed my hands on his shoulders, and said: "If some day you are able to fulfill the conditions that through me God and the community have imposed on you, then the abbey will be open to you to the great joy of us all."

There was no reaction from him. The evening was now cool and three-quarters of the lake lay in shadow. Color was departing and the green of the pine trees became darker and then turned to blackness. I said to Cosmas: "We must go back now. Do you want to spend the night in the guesthouse?"

His head was still bowed down. With a voice full of immense weariness he said: "Thank you, Father. Leave me now."

I traced the sign of the cross on his forehead and then rejoined the road and slowly returned to La Trappe.

Gradually the sky darkened: the clouds no longer scudded across it but were massed together like a flock of sheep that has come to a halt. Was the coldness that I felt merely that of night coming down, or was it something else that pierced my heart and conscience yet again with a sense of failure?

I had hoped with all my heart that Cosmas would give me a positive answer and this time commit himself irrevocably. I now believed that he was capable of it, since his desire to serve God in the Trappist habit was so sincere and long lasting. Why had he refused this commitment? I had to ask this question: had I, once again, bungled my part in the exchange of love between God and Cosmas?

Christ probably took pity on the distress into which this conversation with Cosmas had cast me. Like the Emmaus pilgrims, I felt that I was no longer alone on the road. I relished this accompanying presence for a while and then, my heart burning with love, prayed that the Lord Jesus would go and sit beside Cosmas who, I supposed, was still there by the upper lake, poised between his dream and despair, his brow catching the last rays of the autumn sun.

15

News quickly got round of Cosmas's attempt to reenter the monastery, of our long walk together and our parting on the bank of the upper lake. Even a stretch of country that to all appearances is deserted may contain a number of remarkably alert observers. The tavern keeper who seems to be merely sleeping off his wine before his door, takes it all in with his sharp little eyes and forgets nothing. The woodcutter whom one hasn't actually seen but whose presence could be guessed at from the sounds of his work—the blows of an ax, the whir of an electric saw—has also registered everything, and his mind goes to and fro, from deduction to deduction, like an incisive saw blade. In this case it was most probably one of the farmworkers who was delighted to observe any hint of conflict in the community and who went on to gossip about it and exaggerate it.

We discovered that the strangest rumors about Cosmas were going the rounds.

Folk tales abound in these parts. A landscape broken by valleys and divided by tall hedges, narrow winding streams, farms on lonely hillsides, woodcutters' houses lurking in the depths of the forests, forests that night and day keep watch from the hilltops as though spying on the road below, the lakes surrounded by marshland, frequent mists, secretive manor houses, and monasteries tucked away in a fold of the hills—all this makes Le Perche a fertile soil for the growth of legends. Since I came here more than fifty years ago, there have been so many stories about witches who can cast spells or work miracles and about healers who invoke the devil before mixing beef fat with herbs and crushed grain at the kitchen range.

It was alleged that Cosmas, after I left him, had remained seated on the tree trunk for three days and three nights, as still as a statue. Then he began to prowl around La Trappe like a wild beast. One day he had been spotted here, the next day somewhere else. Every week brought some new and preposterous detail: about the abandoned cottage, said to be haunted, that he had made his lair; about how he fed himself; about the changes in his face and body. You cannot imagine the level of absurdity that was reached. The unfortunate Cosmas was very nearly provided with devilish horns, cloven feet, eyes that gleamed in the dark, not forgetting a whiff of sulfur fumes. It was like a collective hallucination: some managed to avoid it and claimed to be genuinely skeptical; others pretended to believe it; and others again were persuaded that they really did believe it. Mothers forbade their children to go near crossroads where Cosmas had been sighted and kept them indoors after dark.

It was all so irrational and incoherent. We knew that it would take a few months for all interest in the story to fade away, or perhaps less if some other event seized the popular imagination, which was always in search of the slightest incident in a region where nothing very much ever happened.

And yet out of curiosity I was more than once tempted to take an interest in these stories. Had the wild rumors some basis in fact? Had Cosmas remained somewhere near the abbey after I left him? Or did he come back from time to time, impelled by some lingering hope? Whatever the truth might be, it could not amount to a reason for questioning our decision . . .

In short we would have been content to let passage of time ensure that people would grow weary of stories that, for lack of anything else, still seemed to amuse them, were it not that two brothers just back from the fields claimed to have seen Cosmas. They were both suspect witnesses: one of them, Brother Grégoire, was not very bright; the other, Brother Étienne, was extremely shortsighted but never wore his glasses outside the abbey for fear of breaking them. But a few days later two other brothers said that they had glimpsed someone who might have been Cosmas. A woodcutter emerging from the forest shortly after the mysterious form had vanished said that he, too, thought he had recognized Cosmas. There were other bits of evidence, all of them equally untrustworthy.

Father Abbot gave no credence to these rumors. I had given him an account of my conversation with Cosmas. He had agreed with my attitude and considered the matter closed. In his view it was highly likely that some of our neighbors had deliberately set out to confuse the minds of some of the monks, hoping that the rumors would eventually reach La Trappe.

But gradually Father Abbot came to realize that these attempts to make mischief within the abbey were not wholly unsuccessful and that far too many monks were still obsessed with Cosmas. I myself had to admit with considerable shame that I gave way to a stupid hallucination if only for a few seconds. We had just carried to the grave the mortal remains of Brother Théodore, one of those seraphic monks, of whom, in the time of the Fioretti, legend would have alleged that a lily grew out of his breast. We were standing round the patch of freshly dug soil where Théodore lay and saying our farewell prayers. The sun was going down when suddenly, about fifty yards away, just beyond a field of Jerusalem artichokes, I noticed a vague shape that moved slowly against the light of the setting sun. The thought struck me that it must obviously be Cosmas . . .

Father Abbot raised his eyes with the excessive slowness that I was so used to. I met a gaze that I felt would be justifiably severe, but in fact his eyes were relieved by an almost playful twinkle. Dom Philippe said simply: "In that case, Father, the novices are more levelheaded than you are."

Then he dismissed me.

But in chapter the next day he spoke to us without any beating about the bush. He was a tough-minded man of God. He said that all the rumors about Cosmas seemed to him to be pure inventions. The few facts or alleged facts that had come to his notice had all been founded on the shakiest of evidence, and had been blown up and interpreted by third parties whose intentions were not always honorable. The people of the neighborhood had a perfect right to be diverted by such ghost stories, if that was what they wanted, and we shouldn't be surprised or scandalized if they tried to involve us in their self-deception.

"The real scandal," said Father Abbot firmly, "begins when some of us begin to take this tittle-tattle seriously and to be carried away in this infantile manner. What is the point of a life of prayer and penance within the enclosure if we then succumb so uncritically to such nonsense just as readily as those who have to suffer the pressures of the world? And even if there were the slightest basis for these rumors about the comings and goings of Cosmas, they are no longer any concern of ours. The decisions that had to be taken in Cosmas's case have been taken."

He concluded: "I forbid you in the strictest possible way to talk about Cosmas and to exchange so-called information on what he is alleged to be doing, whether among yourselves or with people outside the community. You should go further still: try to forget about him, except to recommend him to the Lord in your prayers."

16

The passage of time and the brisk intervention of Father Abbot soon dissipated the trouble caused in the minds of some of the brethren by the alleged appearances of Cosmas. Popular curiosity, meanwhile, had moved on to other matters: a Polish farmworker had mysteriously vanished a few days after the death of an old woman who lived alone in the most appalling squalor but who was supposed to have hidden wealth. There were no grounds for linking the two events, but racial feeling is deep-rooted and everyone, including the police, was convinced that the Pole had done the deed. They searched every thicket in the forest, every stable and isolated house, every hedge; the locals found this manhunt more exciting than boar hunting. Cosmas receded into the background.

But I couldn't stop thinking about him with any less intensity. God has given me the grace, particularly valuable in religious life, of not being plagued by scruples. I didn't now want to call into question what I had said during our long walk by

the lakes. To oblige Cosmas to make a wholehearted commitment was the only reasonable solution both for him and for the
community: it would have been absurd to make him promise
to have no further difficulties, but it made sense to ask him
whether he could accept our remedies rather than temporary
flight, the only one he knew. But that did not stop me thinking
about his future and praying daily that whatever he did would
be in accordance with his own good and the will of the Lord.

I was surprised and rather worried at not receiving any letters
from him, for writing came easily to him, at times too easily.

Sometimes I imagined that the worst had happened: the
suicide of someone who was trapped, caught between a vocation of which he was morally certain and a set of conditions
that he was unable to accept because he was not sure of being
able to meet them. Had I not incurred a grave responsibility
in giving the impression that he was cornered and, as it were,
caught in a noose? I consoled myself with the thought that
despair was not in Cosmas's character: he had indeed an extraordinary capacity for emerging from disappointments that
seemed to point toward total collapse and to refashion another
mirage, to set off on a new tack, with undaunted and astonishing optimism.

For that reason I thought it unlikely that he would ever give
up the idea of being a monk or that he would seek to realize it
anywhere other than at La Trappe. Either course would have

been a natural solution to his problem. But neither fit in with Cosmas's character. I sometimes wondered whether he had failed to respond to a providential vocation. Against all likelihood, I further wondered whether his unreasonable behavior, this contradiction between a constantly repeated certainty and an inclination to take flight in times of difficulty, was not the sign of a frustrated vocation rather than a mistaken one. But in the secrecy of prayer I had no clearer answers to the questions I put to God in Cosmas's absence than I had received when he was here.

Such thoughts went round and round in my mind endlessly, and filled me with darkness, sadness, and foreboding. They failed to account for Cosmas's continued silence. And this period would have been a time of deep inner distress were it not that my two novices, who had taken the names of Bruno and Bonaventure, brought me the human and spiritual consolation that I needed: the experience of a normal growth in religious life where the obstacles were familiar enough.

Eventually I received news about Cosmas in a most unexpected way: a visit from Dominique, our former agricultural student.

One Sunday afternoon toward the end of August, almost ten months after my last conversation with Cosmas, a brother brought a message to say that I was wanted in the lodge. There I found Dominique, who had driven down from Paris by car.

He still had his wonderful smile and a face tanned by the sun during Mediterranean holidays, but he looked unusually serious. He said: "Father, can I talk to you at some length? It's about Jean-Cosmas."

This double name, which he alone used, uttered in his characteristic accent, took me back to the time two years before when Cosmas had returned in joy and in hope after his first absence.

The weather was sultry and the roads dusty: there's an old proverb in Le Perche that says that "the weather has sticky feet." I led Dominique toward my office, which was at least well aired if not exactly comfortable. There I left him for a few minutes. I wanted to let Father Abbot know about this visit, to ask his advice, and to be dispensed from attending office if the length of the conversation demanded it. We now knew the illness from which Father Abbot suffered, and he seemed in pain and looked very weary: it may be that he had been unable to get to sleep, perhaps for several nights. He lifted his arms in the air in a gesture of hopelessness and said that I knew the facts of the case as well as he did.

When I got back to my office I found Dominique, his hands clasped behind his back, standing before the crucifix, which he was contemplating with a look that combined perplexity and awe. I invited him to sit down.

"A few months ago," he said, "I had a letter from Jean-Cosmas, who by then was living in Paris. Since I go there fairly often, we've met frequently and talked a great deal."

As though embarrassed, he paused a moment, and then went on: "Now I thought I had to come and see you."

He spoke without a break for about an hour. It was evident that he had carefully prepared what he had to say. Many of the details he mentioned seemed to me to be irrelevant, but no doubt he thought otherwise and I understood that it was better not to interrupt him. I have to admit, too, that as a northerner, I found his spontaneous rhetoric and its accompanying gestures rather sympathetic.

Dominique told me first of all about Cosmas's family. His father had died after womanizing until his last months. His mother had retired to a house near Beaune run by nuns: she was no longer in her right mind. Cosmas had tried to get in touch with his brother again, but their meeting had merely proved the depth of the gulf that now separated them. Their only common ground was childhood memories that neither of them wanted to dwell upon. By working tremendously hard, the elder brother was becoming highly successful in what is conventionally called a brilliant career. He had married a woman who was beautiful, cold, and intelligent, who gave him no children. Religious convictions and practice meant nothing to him. Meanwhile, the younger sister, on whose birth Cosmas had vainly pinned great hopes for the reconciliation of his parents, was being looked after by an aunt who lived in England and who had sent the girl to a convent school not far from London.

Through a friend of his father, Cosmas had found work as a sales supervisor in a firm that made veterinary medicines. He spent three or four days a week away from Paris. He seemed to be successful in his profession. The power of conviction that he possessed made him a good salesman. But apart from his work, Cosmas lived like a hermit, as far as Dominique could tell. He had rented an extremely modest room from a retired couple. In Paris and on the road he went to Mass every day and spent the evenings in meditation, prayer, and reading. On Sundays and when possible on Saturday afternoons he helped the priests in the parish where he had worked before.

I didn't interrupt Dominique. I'd always seen him in perpetual movement but now he remained stiff and upright in his chair. Only the hands filled out and orchestrated his words. The sentences flowed with the sort of rhythm one finds in Muslim prayer. He had a slightly singsong voice, and sometimes stressed the end of his sentences, while at other times leaving them trailing in the air like questions. A sudden change of tone made it clear when he was embarking on a digression or backtracking in his story to recall some forgotten detail.

Then he came to the crucial point. Having described Cosmas's present way of life, he paused, looked up at the ceiling, screwed up his mouth in his usual way, and then looked me directly in the eyes as though to gauge the impact of what he was going to say: "You know," he said, "that Cosmas has not abandoned the idea of coming back here?"

I'd expected this. I enquired whether Dominique was expressing his own opinion or whether this was a message from his friend. He answered: "Jean-Cosmas knows what I am doing."

I made the question more precise: "Who took the initiative?"

Dominique sketched a vague gesture, from which I concluded that the responsibility was shared.

It seemed clear that Dominique knew the reasons that had led Father Abbot and me to refuse to readmit Cosmas after his last departure, and that he also knew the conditions attached to his eventual return to the community. So without more ado I asked: "Is Cosmas now capable of committing himself in a definitive way? If something or someone lets him down, will he be able simply to offer his disappointment to God instead of letting it add to his inner difficulties? And if he had another breakdown, will he be able to pull himself together without leaving La Trappe?"

Dominique spent some time collecting his thoughts. In the freshness and shade of the office, the only hint of the sultry sun was the ray of light coming through the glass panel of the door, which cast light on the corridor wall; the silence was broken only by the sound of church bells. Then Dominique resumed his story, more hesitantly this time, with frequent glances at me as though he were seeking my response to and approval of what he was saying. His attitude seemed to be: this is what I think and feel, but am I right to think and feel as I do?

"In my opinion," he said, "Cosmas has broken through into a new stage. He is now fully aware that he will always have to suffer from the gap between what he expects from people and situations and what he actually finds in them. But I think he's banished for good what used to be his immediate reaction during his first stay here: the idea that people and situations would change to fit in with his dreams."

"I've already noted this change in him," I told Dominique. "But it's not enough for Cosmas to know that in such difficulties he needs to act on himself rather than on others. He still has got to show that he can do it without leaving the abbey, without, as he puts it, leaving so that he can come to the surface and breathe again."

Dominique pondered this for a moment. Then he replied that neither he nor anyone else, not even Cosmas himself, could give an absolutely certain guarantee on this point. But he thought that Cosmas's store of goodwill and his perseverance justified another trial attempt. He added that Cosmas had declared that his affection for and confidence in me had been strengthened by his absence. He had given Dominique the same explanation for his flight that he had given me; he knew that he had put himself gravely in the wrong by the manner of his departure; and I would certainly now find that he was more inclined to take my advice rather than follow his own immediate impulses.

I watched Dominique as he spoke. It was rather strange that a monk and a novice master, who at that time had already had fifteen years of monastic life, should be consulting a young unbeliever on the spiritual destiny of a novice. But the affection we both had for Cosmas put us on the same wavelength. Evening began to fall. The patch of sunlight on the wall outside had gone. From time to time one saw the shadowy outline of a passing monk. What little light there was came through the glass-panel door of my office and by now it was almost dark. But I saw no reason to believe that we would have understood each other any better if the light had been on and we had been able to see each other.

I came back to the crucial question: "Is Cosmas now able to undertake and be faithful to the undertaking I asked of him by the upper lake, that he would once and for all give up the idea that a temporary absence was the remedy for his moods?"

Dominique replied with some vigor: "If Jean-Cosmas commits himself, he will keep his word."

I pressed home the question: "But is he ready to commit himself?"

Dominique seemed to hesitate. As though debating the question within himself, he said, with eyes cast down: "Obviously, Jean-Cosmas is rather scrupulous. If he had the slightest doubt . . ."

Then he raised his eyes, looked me straight in the face, and said in a voice that surprised me, moved me, and made me want to smile—it was almost the tone of an elder son talking to a rather wayward younger brother: "Forgive me, Father, but are you so sure that so much importance should be attached to this commitment? I mean, that he should or should not agree to a certain form of words? I can assure you that apart from his work he leads the life of a monk. I can also assure you that he talks constantly of his desire to return to La Trappe, and of his certainty that he will return, and that he says this with great calm and without getting overexcited. I know nothing about these matters, as you realize, but as an outsider I find it difficult to believe that Cosmas's vocation is not serious."

I prayed intensely as I listened to Dominique. The bells announced that the evening meal was over: I hadn't even noticed the bells that meant that it was about to begin. I felt pulled this way and that by contradictory thoughts. Of course, a novice is not bound by his vows, even temporary ones. But Cosmas was not like any other novice. We had felt obliged to send him away from the abbey; and the second time he had fled . . . Commitment is so self-evidently needed in a religious that I couldn't see us welcoming him back again after two absences without insisting on a statement of intention at the very least . . . And yet the idea that had been haunting me in the last few months now came home to me and inclined me to agree with Dominique: although appearances were against him and he seemed to lack the necessary dispositions to realize it, Cosmas's vocation was genuine enough; and we had no right to say that he was quite incapable of adapting to the Cistercian life . . . At the same time I realized with the utmost clarity all the risks that Cosmas's return would entail: another disappointment for him and more trouble for the community . . .

Why was it that prayer never brought me light and clarity where Cosmas was concerned? Why did I feel thrown back on my own resources? And how was it that on that evening, I, for whom obedience had become second nature, who had always shared with Father Abbot the responsibility for dealing with the difficult problems raised by Cosmas and who had always been helped by his penetrating understanding and sound judgment—I, who in talking to him of Cosmas had experienced the great joy of glimpsing in Dom Philippe the sensitive and vulnerable human being that he concealed from us—how was it that on this occasion, whereas only two hours before my first thought was to warn him of the arrival of Dominique and ask his advice, I felt no need to consult Father Abbot before giving Dominique the answer that I had to give?

I smiled at him: "Tell him that he has a good advocate and that we are prepared to let him try again."

I felt bound to add: "But this is only because we now think that he is ready to fulfill the conditions we laid down."

Dominique was in a hurry to get back to Paris and refused the meal I offered him. I went with him to the lodge. The bell was ringing for Compline, which concludes with the Salve Regina and sets us on our way toward a restful night.

Next morning, I went to Father Abbot's office, kneeled down before him, and asked his forgiveness for the presumption and imprudence with which I had taken upon myself the decision to give Cosmas another chance.

Father Abbot passed no judgment on what I had done. He indicated that I should rise and, without looking at me, asked me to tell him what had happened. He listened with his usual intentness to my account of this long conversation and of the reasons that had led to my decision. When I had done, without opening his eyes, he said rather curtly but with more weariness and concern than reproach: "Very well, Father, let the grace of God take its course . . ."

17

Several weeks went by without any news of Cosmas.

Autumn had come again, and it was almost as glorious as in the previous year. When I happened to walk in the places where I had been with Cosmas for the last time, my soul and heart felt carried away with a sort of impatience and at times an anxiety which only prayer could calm.

At last I received a letter from him. As I read it through, I felt his presence just as ever before. He apologized for not having gotten in touch earlier, but he had recently had a lot of extra work; I smiled at the idea that he had probably, in his usual way, waited a long time before deciding to act. He thanked me for the answer conveyed through the intervention of Dominique. This had touched him deeply and brought him a joy that he revealed discreetly and soberly, as was his wont, and yet he didn't seem to realize how remarkable, given the manner of his departure, this permission to return to La Trappe really was. Once again he said how certain he felt about his vocation, and how he needed to answer faithfully the call that he had never ceased to hear.

"If you hadn't agreed to Dominique's request," he wrote, "I would not have been put off. I would have gone on praying and waiting for as long as was needed to convince you and earn your forgiveness."

Finally he explained that he had to give his employer three months' notice, and said that he would scrupulously fulfill all his obligations and leave everything in order. That meant that he could not come to La Trappe before the end of the year, or more likely before the first weeks of the new year.

"But," he went on, "I am with you already in my heart and my thoughts and my prayer, and have never ceased to be with you."

The orchards, hedges, and forest continued to blaze with color long after the feast of St. Martin. December, Christmas, and the first weeks of January were misty but mild. The life of the community reflected the weather: nothing very outstanding happened; there was no particular mood to record. I was sometimes reminded of the sense of grayness and routine that Cosmas had found so dispiriting. And yet every day prayer and praise, acts of renunciation, humble tasks accomplished in obedience, minor victories over doubt or tepidity, repugnances mastered, clashes of mood or superficial irritations overcome by charity—all these rose up to the Lord. And God, who had called us to this life, no doubt found them good.

But winter suddenly came in with a vengeance on the feast of St. Agnes. Snowstorms alternated with periods of dry cold when, day and night, the frozen sky seemed both pitiless and transparent. Everything froze over—first the puddles in the ruts of the tracks, then the ponds, and finally the lakes: the few boys who were allowed by their parents to go to school spent their time skimming stones across the ice before sliding recklessly over it. Very soon the whole area was buried beneath a layer of snow deeper than anyone had ever seen in our hills, which hardly ever rise above a few hundred feet. Farms were cut off, roads made impassable or entirely blocked by snow-drifts; the cattle in the fields suffered from hunger and thirst.

Our minds were entirely taken up with practical matters. On Father Abbot's instructions, we tried to heat some of the rooms, but apart from open grates with chimneys that had never been used—we get through ordinary winters without needing to light a fire—the abbey had no means of heating. Despite our efforts, the temperature remained arctic, and the beds in the infirmary, the only reasonably warm place, were always filled. Washbasins and sinks were adorned with stalactites. Unprotected pipes burst. Several times a day we had to break the ice to allow the cattle to drink.

I hadn't forgotten that Cosmas was due back. But Cosmas and everything connected with him seemed to belong to another world on which I looked as though through a plate-glass window. I began really to worry about his delayed arrival as winter ended early in March.

Although the weather was now mild, the snow and ice took a long time to melt. Patches of dirty white snow clung to the hedgerows or lingered in folds of the hills or on the shadow side of slopes: they held off the onslaughts of a thousand tiny, brownish rivulets that gnawed away at their edges. The water in the ditches flowed beneath a layer of thick ice.

It was about then that one of our farmhands, a tall fellow with a slight limp who did a bit of dawn poaching, discovered Cosmas. The body was in the bottom of a gully just below the road that leads to La Trappe and not far from the Aspres crossroads. All that emerged from the snow was part of a sock and a trousered leg, but the farmworker, who had the eyes of a hunter and was trained to notice the slightest trace of an animal, spotted them immediately. He went down the slope, removed the snow, and pulled: the body came out in one piece, still stiff from the cold, and unharmed except for part of the neck and face that the animals had got at.

The man limped his way back to the abbey as fast as he could go, was out of breath by the time he reached the lodge, but was delighted to be the bearer of such sensational and macabre news. During the rest of the day there was great activity around the body, which was guarded by two gendarmes: the coroner fussed about, and there were also experts and the police doctor. Toward nightfall Father Abbot, who was now barely able to walk, was driven to the scene and after a long discussion with the coroner obtained permission to remove the body to the abbey and to bury it, provisionally at least, in the parish cemetery, though only after a few more tests had been made on it the following morning. When Dom Philippe later decided that burial would take place at La Trappe and not at Soligny, it didn't seem to him important to let the authorities know.

The inquest lasted several weeks. No certain conclusions were reached as to the circumstances of Cosmas's death, except that according to the experts it had happened some weeks before.

Neither the bus drivers on the route between Aigle and Mortagne nor the local taxi drivers could remember having taken anyone answering to Cosmas's description during the winter. Cosmas had come by train as far as Aigle: but had he then tried to walk the twenty kilometers to La Trappe? That seemed unlikely in the sort of weather we'd been having. The most likely theory was that he had hitched a lift to the crossroads where the road branches off for the abbey. But the driver who brought him to the crossroads was never discovered.

Nor did we discover how Cosmas had died. The doctors found no traces of violence on the body and were unable to offer any certain diagnosis. Had Cosmas fainted? Had he slipped down into the gully and, cold and half stifled by snow, been unable to get up? Had someone attacked him? But who and why? It was true that his suitcase had disappeared, but anyone might have taken it and anyway it contained nothing of value. His wallet was still there in the inside pocket of his jacket: it still contained a considerable sum of money that he probably intended to donate to the abbey.

One point was definitely established with the help of Cosmas's landlady: the date on which he had left Paris. That suggested that we could with all probability conclude that he had died in the first week of February when there had been an almost unbroken series of snowstorms: it wasn't at all surprising that a body falling into the gully should have been covered over completely in a single night.

I wrote immediately to Dominique. He arrived a month later: he had been traveling a great deal and my letter had taken time to catch up with him.

He confirmed for us how deeply moved Cosmas had been when informed that we had agreed to take him back in the abbey: there had been no words, just a prolonged, almost febrile, handshake. He also confirmed that on the same day Cosmas had said that it would take him a longish time to fulfill his obligations and wind up his business affairs before returning to the abbey. However, he had gathered that Cosmas intended to leave Paris toward the end of December or right at the start of January rather than in February—and this fitted in with what Cosmas had written in his last letter. But since his professional duties had kept him away from Paris, he had not seen Cosmas for several months, and he could not explain why he had left later than foreseen nor say in what mood he had set off for La Trappe.

A notebook found in Cosmas's pocket gave us the addresses of the members of his family. Father Abbot wrote briefly to each of them to let them know of the accidental death, but without going into details, and he added that the burial had taken place in the abbey cemetery. The superior of the retreat house where Cosmas's mother dragged out her obscure life replied on her behalf. Using the stiff, formal style at that time customary in convents, Mother Superior noted the tactful way in which providence had arranged that Cosmas's mother was no longer well enough to suffer from the sad news. The elder brother sent a telegram in which he expressed his regrets rather impersonally and offered to pay our expenses. The younger sister, who was finishing her studies in England, was the only one to come and see, the following summer, the place where her brother had lived. I saw her in the guest parlor and did my best to answer the flood of questions she put to me. She was a tall girl, well built with rather bony features, who was probably like her father, whereas Cosmas—he had often claimed—took after his mother. But I saw in her many of the psychological features that I had noticed in her brother. She had been ten years old when he left for his military service and then for La Trappe, and so she hardly knew him; but she had retained a sketchy and idealized image of him; and her idea of monks and religious life was, with added naïveté, the same that Cosmas had when he first came here.

I had to admit that the detailed circumstances of his death remained and probably always would remain an impenetrable mystery. I stressed the fact—rather more strongly than I was actually convinced of—that Father Abbot's decision to have Cosmas buried in the monastic cemetery clearly signified that Cosmas had fulfilled his vocation and belonged to the community. At the end of the conversation she expressed a desire to pray by the grave of her brother. I had to refuse her: the cemetery is part of the enclosure where women are not allowed. But I promised to send her a photograph of the grave if Father Abbot agreed.

The discovery of the corpse had stimulated a fresh crop of fantastic rumors in the neighborhood. Rural France is still obsessed with wolves, and they were alleged to have caused the wounds on the face and neck of Cosmas: but it was obvious that they were the work of those tiny carnivores that abound in the forest and feed on living prey or the dead flesh of larger animals. But popular imagination invented still wilder explanations for the tragic death of Cosmas: he was supposed to have made a pact with Satan and then broken one of its clauses by straying too near to the abbey in a snowstorm, whereupon the devil struck him down dead.

But these fantastic stories, despite the efforts of some of our neighbors who were determined to disturb the peace of the abbey, had no effect on the community itself. The excitement caused in the minds of a few monks by the alleged sightings of Cosmas had given way to a bitter sense of remorse. The taciturn reserve that had been the attitude of the majority of the brethren concerning the burial of Cosmas by the apse of the abbey church was partly a way of saying that things were now back to normal but it also expressed a certain weariness. And when, despite this general mood, Father Abbot had ordered the burial to take place in the cemetery at La Trappe and when the bearers of the body had filled in the grave with spadefuls of clay, most of the monks were also burying the memory of troubles now past. Monastic life needs serenity: serenity now duly returned after being briefly disturbed by the unfortunate episode of Cosmas.

But I could never regard the life and death of my former novice as a closed file, now over and done with. My thinking and my prayer were still haunted, more than they ought to have been, by unanswerable questions and hazardous theories that pounded against my soul like the last waves of a storm that refuses to die down. If Cosmas's vocation was not genuine, why was he never made aware of it? Why had he never really taken any notice of the warnings of Father Abbot and myself, though he was neither proud nor rebellious? Why was it that both of us—and myself much more than Dom Philippe—had been so doubtful and hesitant, even though Cosmas's case was, alas, all too familiar in spiritual literature? Why was it that despite Cosmas's errors of judgment and his running away the second time—there is no other word for it—I nevertheless in my heart never completely rejected the idea that Cosmas's vocation was genuine, to such an extent that Dominique had little difficulty in persuading me of its authenticity? And if Cosmas, as he was convinced to the end, really was destined to serve God in the habit of a Cistercian, why had the grace to realize this vocation been withheld from him? What meaning should be given to this strange death, so close to La Trappe, at the very moment when he was on the verge of being readmitted? And if Cosmas had once more taken his place in the community, what would have happened to him and what would have been our relationship with him?

One Sunday afternoon I was in the scriptorium, still obsessed by these questions and distracted from my reading by them, contemplating the splendid portrait that Rigaud somewhat surprisingly painted of the Abbé de Rancé, when Father Abbot appeared and invited me to follow him.

Dom Philippe was thinner than ever. Once a week he was driven by Brother Sébastien to the hospital at Alençon—on these occasions his sensitive driving style became even gentler. There the abbot was bombarded with cobalt rays, which at that time were the latest thing in cancer treatment. But the illness was getting worse and one could see that he had to bear with much suffering.

He walked slowly and I, round and awkward, followed the tall, hieratic figure. We went past the vegetable garden and sat down on a wooden bench where the orchard began: at that time it ran along the bank of de Rancé Lake, the lowest lying of the lakes dug by the monks of old to drain the countryside. Tourists don't know about it, since the mass of the abbey buildings hides it from the road and it can be reached only through the enclosure. As you have seen, it is smaller than Chaumont Lake, nor does it have the air of mystery possessed by the upper lake—before the taverns were allowed in—where I had my last conversation with Cosmas. The discreet charm of de Rancé Lake inspires the sense of peace, isolation, and silence that the great reformer of La Trappe, who gave his name to the lake, wanted to reintroduce into this place.

Spring that day seemed lyrical with the tender freshness of newly awakened life. The cherry trees were a foam of white blossom. Black-headed tomtits chased each other in their wild zigzag flight and quarreled noisily over the worms and grubs they found among the young shoots. The sky seemed to tremble out of sheer joy, like a lake rippled by the wind.

Dom Philippe had found it difficult to get his breath back. Then he said: "Father Roger . . ."

Normally he called me Father. I interpreted this use of my religious name as a prelude to a conversation of a more intimate nature than usual. I looked at him. With that characteristic movement of the upper body, he turned toward me, his face ravaged and yet refined by suffering, and slowly opened his eyelids, revealing the light blue eyes that were now reddened at the rim.

"Father Roger," he went on, "I have only a few more months, perhaps weeks, to live. I know that after my death the brethren will elect you abbot. I am very happy about this choice: it is the best possible for the good of the community. I shall pray for you in this world and the next; and I will offer up my sufferings for you, till the last moment. Being abbot is a heavy responsibility."

I told him from the depths of my heart how unworthy I felt of such high office. If I needed any convincing on that score, the events of the last few months were enough to prove it . . .

"You're thinking of Cosmas," he said.

It was an assertion, not a question. Dom Philippe was so possessed by the Holy Spirit that his look, like the light of God, seemed to pierce through me and rob me of my defenses.

He said that he knew—more precisely, he saw—the questions that were on my mind. But he considered that they were now irrelevant. We had been responsible for Cosmas: now God had taken him into his hands and that should be enough for us to cast aside all worry and to stop futile self-questionings.

"Yet it remains true," Father Abbot continued, "that the Cosmas affair still worries me as I know it troubles you. Although you and I have very different characters, we have in common that we both like to act decisively. Should we make mistakes in the exercise of our various offices, they will spring not from too much hesitation but from excessive self-confidence. Perhaps God simply wanted us to learn a lesson in modesty by presenting us with this unusual case, and to remind us that he alone knows what is in the human heart."

I remained silent, sensing that Dom Philippe had not reached the end of his thoughts. He went on: "Perhaps also the Lord wanted to remind us of something else: his judgments are not ours; what counts in his eyes is the acceptance as much as the accomplishment. He did not want Isaac to die, but he wanted Abraham to be prepared to sacrifice his son out of obedience. When faced with a vocation of whatever kind, we try; we have to try to evaluate it by taking into account the dispositions and the likelihood of success. We have no right, as mere human beings, to encourage someone to adopt a way of life that he seems incapable of fulfilling. And the loftier and the more ambitious the vocation, the more prudence and rigor should be brought to the assessment of the candidate's aptitudes. It is right that we should be most severe and sensitive in our screening of those who want to dedicate themselves to the exclusive service of God. When we questioned Cosmas's vocation, when we first tested it and then discouraged it, we were exercising our ordinary human responsibility, you as novice master and I as abbot.

"But God uses other scales on which our poor human achievements probably don't count for very much.

"The vocation of a Bach or a Mozart seems to be beyond all question because of the wonderful music they produced. But in the sight of God, have they any more value than that of any other musician, without their talent and grace, who has heard an inner call and tried to answer it until death? Those who suffer from this gap between their aspirations and their attainments—and whom we cruelly call failures—are perhaps less deceived about their talent than we imagine. But in their eyes the sense of inadequacy, of getting nowhere, and their failures, do not relieve them of the responsibility to keep on trying, unweariedly though in vain . . ."

Father Abbot paused again, as though he wanted to sharpen his thoughts still further, and then he went on: "Has not this kind of fidelity, sustained neither by dispositions nor success, an altogether special value—provided it really is fidelity to an inner voice and is not merely the result of pride or obstinacy?

"Wasn't Cosmas much more lucid in his own case than we thought he was? Didn't he very soon understand how difficult it would be for him to become a good monk, as his second departure proved so convincingly? He knew that he was weak, utopian, easily disappointed, and he thought that he couldn't take a grip on himself again except by going away. But even so, perhaps he was onto the truth when he said that despite everything God continued to call him to his service. We thought his obstinate desire to return here showed a complete lack of judgment, but perhaps it involved great courage."

I listened to Father Abbot, utterly fascinated. Now I knew for sure that he had considered all the questions about Cosmas that had obsessed me—and that he was speaking as much for his own sake as for mine.

He was a little out of breath and I suggested that we should go back to his office. He said no with a brief, dismissive gesture, and after a few moments of recollection, as though once more gathering his thoughts before sharing them with me, he went on: "Isn't it a good thing that occasionally, when God so wills it, there should be instances of an enduring vocation within a religious community, despite the lack of natural dispositions?

"You see, Father Roger, we monks forget how privileged we are in having so much time to test our vocations. Quite clearly the exceptional seriousness of our commitment to God demands that we should be prudent in this matter. But our constitutions provide for at least five years before final vows. How many people are there in the world who can spend five years thinking and studying before committing themselves to marriage, for example? And what can they do when they find that they were mistaken, and that they have not the right dispositions to live with someone to whom they once felt called, when the choice comes down to this: either breaking their commitment or fidelity? A fidelity against winds and tempests that eventually, by the grace of God, enables the incompatibility to be overcome, and produces truth where once there was error. A fidelity that guarantees the reality of a vocation where the aptitude for it was lacking.

"Wasn't Cosmas the brother in Christ of all those who have set off on a wrong path, with a mistaken commitment, and yet have remained faithful?"

Father Abbot fell silent. Then his face was suffused by a smile in which one could read, superabundantly, intelligence, love, and thankfulness.

"If that is true," he said, "then the fact that our Brother Cosmas died when he did reveals the Lord's infinite mercy toward him. He died when he was on his way to La Trappe yet again, and thus gave further proof of his fidelity; but he died before he had to face his weakness yet again, to our distress, and his own.

"Once more, God reminds us that he knows infinitely better than we do . . ."

The pain came, so suddenly and stabbingly that I saw Father Abbot cling to the bench so hard that his fingernails went into the wood. Tears formed in the corner of his blood-shot eyes. He did not flinch. When the pain was less intense, he went on—and in these words he gathered together in the same hope Cosmas, himself, me, and all those like you, my dear friend, who know the torment of restlessness—". . . that he knows better than we do the way by which each one of us can find peace."

Tignes, March 1975
La Trappe, September 1975
Paris, March 1977

Questions for Reflection and Discussion

Use the following questions as guides to deeper individual understanding of the novel or for group discussion.

1. The novel begins at the end of the story, with Cosmas's burial within the monastery. Why did the author construct the novel this way? How does this affect the way you read the story?

2. We learn the name of the narrator, Father Roger, at the very end of the book. Why did the author withhold this information for so long? Why does he finally divulge it?

3. Father Roger (and the author) tells his story with a subtly evangelistic purpose in mind. The person hearing the story is an unbeliever (p. 122). How do you think an unbeliever would receive this story? What would this person learn from it?

4. Father Roger takes great pains to dispel myths about monastic life. What did you learn about the life of monks from this novel?

5. Cosmas is shocked by the "worldly" way in which the monks conduct their practical affairs. "I expected to find a greater difference between those who remain in the world and those who spend long hours in prayer," he says (p. 91). Father Roger refutes this notion. Is Father Roger correct? Is Cosmas entirely wrong to expect that those specially consecrated to God behave differently?

6. The abbot and Father Roger, two very experienced monks, are baffled by Cosmas. How would you sum up his problem, which lies at the heart of the novel?

7. Father Roger says that people with Cosmas's problem need "disillusionment without despair." They need "to learn to see others and situations as they really are and to regain a sense of their responsibility for their own fate" (p. 153). What do you think of this remark? Does Cosmas achieve this by the end of his life?

8. At the end of the novel, the abbot says that Cosmas's problem is not unique. It's the dilemma of everyone "who suffer[s] from this gap between their aspirations and their attainments. . . . In their eyes the sense of inadequacy, of getting nowhere, and their failures, do not relieve them of the responsibility to keep on trying" (p. 224). Comment on this observation.

9. A question lies at the heart of the novel: Was God calling Cosmas to a vocation at La Trappe? What is your answer?

10. The full title of the novel is *Cosmas or the Love of God.* How does the story show the love of God?

About the Author

Pierre de Calan was born in Paris in 1911. In his childhood he spent summers in the village of Bonsmoulins, in Normandy, not far from the famous monastery La Trappe at Soligny. He visited La Trappe many times in later life. He faithfully describes the monastery and its setting in his only novel, *Cosmas or the Love of God*.

Calan's education was in business, not literature, and he had a successful career as a banker and businessman, eventually becoming president of Barclays Bank in France. *Cosmas* created a stir in French literary circles when Calan published it at age sixty-six. To a critic surprised that a businessman could write such a polished novel, he said, "A man who lives only for his work lives only a half life." Others were impressed that a married layman with six children and eighteen grandchildren could write about monastic life so authentically and convincingly. One of these was the abbot of La Trappe himself, who congratulated Calan on *Cosmas* and declared him "an honorary monk and novice master."

Pierre de Calan died in 1993.

Peter Hebblethwaite (1930–1994) was a British journalist and author whose career featured distinguished reporting from the Vatican. His books include *In the Vatican, John XXIII: Pope of the Century, Georges Bernanos, Theology of the Church, The Runaway Church,* and *The Year of Three Popes.*

LOYOLA CLASSICS

Catholics	Brian Moore	0-8294-2333-8	$11.95
Cosmas of the Love of God	Pierre de Calan	0-8294-2395-8	$12.95
Dear James	Jon Hassler	0-8294-2430-X	$13.95
The Devil's Advocate	Morris L. West	0-8294-2156-4	$12.95
Do Black Patent Leather Shoes Really Reflect Up?	John R. Powers	0-8294-2143-2	$12.95
The Edge of Sadness	Edwin O'Connor	0-8294-2123-8	$13.95
Helena	Evelyn Waugh	0-8294-2122-X	$12.95
In This House of Brede	Rumer Godden	0-8294-2128-9	$13.95
The Keys of the Kingdom	A. J. Cronin	0-8294-2334-6	$13.95
The Last Catholic in America	John R. Powers	0-8294-2130-0	$12.95
Mr. Blue	Myles Connolly	0-8294-2131-9	$11.95
North of Hope	Jon Hassler	0-8294-2357-5	$13.95
Saint Francis	Nikos Kazantzakis	0-8294-2129-7	$13.95
The Silver Chalice	Thomas Costain	0-8294-2350-8	$13.95
Things as They Are	Paul Horgan	0-8294-2332-X	$12.95
The Unoriginal Sinner and the Ice-Cream God	John R. Powers	0-8294-2429-6	$12.95
Vipers' Tangle	François Mauriac	0-8294-2211-0	$12.95

Available at your local bookstore, or visit **www.loyolabooks.org**
or call **800.621.1008** to order.

Readers,

We'd like to hear from you! What other classic Catholic novels would you like to see in the Loyola Classics series? Please e-mail your suggestions and comments to **loyolaclassics@loyolapress.com** or mail them to:

Loyola Classics
Loyola Press
3441 N. Ashland Avenue
Chicago, IL 60657

A Special Invitation

Loyola Press invites you to become one of our Loyola Press Advisors! Join our unique online community of people willing to share with us their thoughts and ideas about Catholic life and faith. By sharing your perspective, you will help us improve our books and serve the greater Catholic community.

From time to time, registered advisors are invited to participate in online surveys and discussion groups. Most surveys will take less than ten minutes to complete. Loyola Press will recognize your time and efforts with gift certificates and prizes. Your personal information will be held in strict confidence. Your participation will be for research purposes only, and at no time will we try to sell you anything.

Please consider this opportunity to help Loyola Press improve our products and better serve you and the Catholic community. To learn more or to join, visit **www.SpiritedTalk.org** and register today.

—The Loyola Press Advisory Team